Praise

"A sweet romance with characters
who only want the best for one another."
—*RT Book Reviews* on "Her Christmas Family"
in *Mail-Order Christmas Brides*

"A sweet, romantic novel,
with memorable characters."
—*RT Book Reviews* on *Snowflake Bride*

"This is a beautiful love story between two people
from different stations in life, or so it appears.
The characters are balanced and well thought out
and the storyline flows nicely."
—*RT Book Reviews* on *Patchwork Bride*

Praise for Janet Tronstad

"This great story filled with kindness,
understanding and love is sure to please."
—*RT Book Reviews* on
"Christmas Stars for Dry Creek,"
in *Mail-Order Christmas Brides*

"Elizabeth is a wonderful, caring character,
a strong-willed woman with tenderness for a
motherless child. Jake is a gentle giant,
and their love story is full of Christmas joy."
—*RT Book Reviews* on *Calico Christmas at Dry Creek*

"Janet Tronstad's quirky small town
and witty characters will add warmth and joy
to your holiday season."
—*RT Book Reviews* on
"Christmas Bells for Dry Creek,"
in *Mistletoe Courtship*

JILLIAN HART

grew up on her family's homestead, where she helped raise cattle, rode horses and scribbled stories in her spare time. After earning her English degree from Whitman College, she worked in travel and advertising before selling her first novel. When Jillian isn't working on her next story, she can be found puttering in her rose garden, curled up with a good book or spending quiet evenings at home with her family.

JANET TRONSTAD

grew up on her family's farm in central Montana and now lives in Pasadena, California, where she is always at work on her next book. She has written more than thirty books, many of them set in the fictitious town of Dry Creek, Montana, where the men spend the winters gathered around the potbellied stove in the hardware store and the women make jelly in the fall.

JILLIAN HART
JANET TRONSTAD

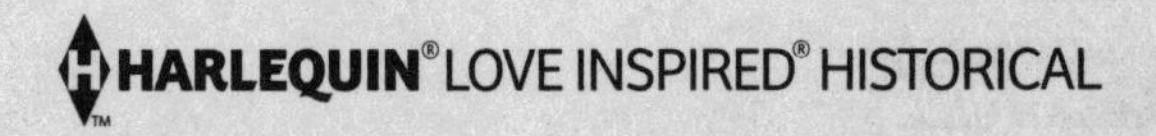

Recycling programs for this product may not exist in your area.

™ LOVE INSPIRED BOOKS

ISBN-13: 978-0-373-82991-0

This edition published by arrangement with Love Inspired Books.

www.Harlequin.com

Printed in U.S.A.

CONTENTS

CHRISTMAS HEARTS

Jillian Hart

To Jenny Blake, from Janet and Jillian.
Meeting you face-to-face in Spokane last May
after being online friends for so many years
was a true blessing. You are a great friend, Jenny.
You have been an inspiration and encouragement
to both of us. We love you. Blessings always.

For You shall enlarge my heart.
—*Psalms* 119:32

Chapter One

Montana Territory
December 20, 1886

The steel *clickety-clack* of the rails slowed as the town of Miles City came into sight. Mercy Jacobs felt her heart catch. Being a mail-order bride was nerve-racking. With every mile and every stop on the route, her new home of Angel Falls came closer and closer.

And so did the reality of meeting the stranger she'd agreed to marry.

"Ma?" Her seven-year-old son fidgeted on the seat beside her, straining to see above the lip of the windowsill to get a better view of the approaching town. "Will Angel Falls be like this one?"

"I don't know, George. Maybe." She smiled past her nervousness. Cole Matheson, the man whose advertisement she'd answered, had written of a friendly railroad town lined with shops, one of which was his own.

"Will it be snowy, too?" Those wide baby-blue eyes filled with a child's hope.

"I reckon so, as your new pa said in his last letter to bundle up, that our first Christmas in Montana Territory was guaranteed to be white."

"Boy, I sure do wanna go out and play in that." George sighed wistfully. As the train chugged a little slower, the view of snowy fields, rolling hills and the snow-mantled roofs of homes clustered along the outskirts of town became crisp, no longer blurred. Easy to soak in and dream a little. George let out a sigh of longing that fogged part of the window. He swiped it away with one hand and watched two children building a snowman in their backyard.

Snow had been hard to come by at their home in North Carolina.

"Miles City, next stop!" The conductor's voice carried above the conversations of passengers in the crowded car, packed with folks traveling to be with family for the holiday.

"Well, that's me." Maeve Flanagan turned around in her seat to smile back at Mercy. The small child seated beside her peered out the window, too. "This is as far as we go."

"Are you nervous? You look nervous. Why, you're absolutely pale." Mercy leaned forward and caught her new friend's hand. They'd met back East when Maeve had boarded the train, a mail-order bride, too. "Take a deep breath."

"I'm fine. It's merely last-minute butterflies." Maeve smiled gently. She was truly striking at nearly six feet tall with beautiful red hair and blue-green eyes. "This is what I've been waiting for this entire journey. Meeting Mr. Noah Miller."

"He'll be everything you've been hoping for, I just know it." Mercy gave Maeve's gloved had a squeeze of encouragement. "Our prayers will be answered."

"We've prayed so often on this trip, surely the Good Lord has heard us." Maeve paused as the train's brakes squealed, making conversation difficult.

The train jerked to a stop, bouncing them in their seats. With the final jerk, all motion ceased. Her time with Maeve had come to an end, but she knew regardless of where their separate paths led them, they would always be friends. Some journeys bound hearts together, and this was one of them.

"Why, it's my two mail-order brides." The conductor, kindly Mr. Blake, paused in the aisle with a sympathetic smile on his round face. He might be a big man and built like on ox, but his heart was bigger. "I've been praying for you lovely ladies. Think of the happiness awaiting you. Why, I can't imagine a thing more romantic. It's almost like a story, first declaring love with each other through your letters and then finding a deeper love when you meet. It must be all poetry and declarations of the heart, like a fairy tale happening just to you. Not only am I a happily married man, so I know what's waiting for you, but it's the Christmas season. Love and happy endings are in the air."

"That's very kind of you," Maeve said gently, as if she wasn't so sure.

Mercy was even less sure. Love was not the reason she had traveled across the country to wed a stranger. She managed a weak smile.

Mr. Blake was not derailed easily. He pulled something from his pockets. He held up two sprigs of handsome green leaves bearing small white berries. A tiny bow of thin velvet ribbon added a festive touch. He grinned widely. "Think of this gift as a wish and a prayer for your happy marriages. For your first kisses on Christmas Day with your new husbands."

"It's mistletoe!" Maeve exclaimed, surprised.

"Oh, thank you." Mercy accepted hers, touched by his thoughtfulness. She wished to say more but he'd already touched his hand to his cap and moved on to help an elderly lady with her valise at the end of the car.

"Bless you, Mr. Blake." Maeve quickly pinned her spray of mistletoe to her collar. "I appreciate the thoughtful wish."

"And you'll have mine, too." Mercy gave Maeve a brief hug. "My prayers for you won't cease."

"Nor will mine for you." With that, Maeve grabbed her young daughter's hand. Little four-year-old Violet was adorable with her dark auburn hair, cherub's face and violet-blue eyes. She looked up at her mother expectantly. Maeve appeared grim as she stepped into the aisle. "Be happy, my friend."

"You, too." She knew how Maeve felt—hollow, knowing that Mr. Blake's wishes for them could not come true. A business arrangement did not a real marriage make. She hugged Maeve and said good-bye to Violet, and they were gone, traipsing down the aisle.

Lord, please grant her happiness in her new marriage, Mercy prayed. *Somehow.*

Her stomach clenched as she settled back into her seat. Soon, it would be her turn to step off the train and meet the man she'd agreed to bind her life to. She smoothed George's flyaway blond hair with her hand. That cowlick always stuck straight up, regardless of what she did. Love for her boy filled her heart.

He was the reason she'd accepted this mail-order situation. Regardless of the type of man Cole Matheson turned out to be, if he was a good father to her son, she would be content. She would endure any disappointments silently and be grateful for a convenient marriage, one without love.

* * *

"Hurry, Pa! We'll be late for the train." Amelia's voice echoed through the dry-goods store, rising above the rustle and din of Christmas customers filling the aisles. The tap of her impatient gait struck like a hammer in uneven raps through the store as she skirted knots of customers and arrowed straight for him. "You promised, Pa. You said you'd keep an eye on the time."

"It's been a busy day." Cole Matheson looked over the top of his reading spectacles, pausing in tallying up Mrs. Lanna Wolf's purchases. He frowned at his daughter. "I haven't heard the train whistle. It's not time yet."

"It's four o'clock." The thirteen-year-old skidded to a stop in front of the counter, her apple cheeks pink from running, her strawberry-blond hair threatening to escape her braids, strands tumbling loose to curl around her face. She looked as if she'd been playing outside with the boys again, with chunks of snow melting in her hair and her blue flannel dress wet in spots. She gestured toward the clock on the wall. "The train's late and so are you. C'mon, we've got to hurry."

"I have to finish helping Mrs. Wolf," he said sternly, for all the good it did. Amelia was used to his ways and wasn't troubled by them. "Now politely apologize to Mrs. Wolf."

"I'm sorry, ma'am." Amelia bobbed in a quick

curtsy. "But my new mother is coming on the train today, and Pa isn't nearly as excited about it as I am."

"Why, this is wonderful news. I hadn't heard." Lanna Wolf smiled gracefully, apparently not troubled by the child's behavior. "Congratulations to you both. What a happy thing to have happen right before Christmas."

"It's my Christmas present," Amelia was quick to explain. "It's the only gift I've asked for every Christmas for three Christmases in a row, and this year I finally wore Pa down. All I had to do was mention how I needed a ma on account of one day soon I'll be needing a corset, and that did it. It changed his mind on the spot."

"I suppose it would." Lanna laughed, seemingly unaware he'd turned two shades brighter than a beet.

"And she's really nice. I read every one of her letters and even wrote her two. She answered them both. I think she'll be a really good ma." Amelia released a dramatic, satisfied sigh. "It'll be the best Christmas present ever."

For his daughter, at least. Cole slipped his glasses higher on his nose and squinted at the column of figures. He doubled-checked his addition and gave Mrs. Wolf her total.

"Just add it to my account, please, Cole." Lanna settled her warm winter hat on her elaborate knot of hair. "Can you deliver this all by supper time?"

"My delivery boy will do his best." He scribbled

a note to the boy on the slip, letting him know that Mrs. Wolf was a priority customer. "Hard to say with the storm moving in."

"Yes, it has the feel of a blizzard out there," Lanna agreed while his daughter bounced up and down in place with her "hurry, Pa" look. "Blessings on your new marriage, and Amelia, I'm so happy you'll have a new mother. What are the odds, I wonder, that she knows what she's getting into?"

"I'll behave, I promise." Amelia's sweet, heart-shaped face shone with earnestness. Amelia was a good girl, but she was rambunctious, regardless of how much she tried otherwise. Perhaps a prim and proper mother's influence would help curb that.

It was his only prayer. Mercy Jacobs came across in her letters as quiet and sensible, and heaven knew that was exactly what his daughter needed. Curbing Amelia's unladylike behavior was the true reason he'd agreed to marry a complete stranger. Every woman he'd approached in town either laughed at his convenient marriage proposition or gaped at him with horror.

At least he hoped Amelia was the reason those women had looked at him that way.

"I'll take over, boss." Middle-aged and efficient Eberta Quinn bustled over in her sensible brown frock. "I'll finish wrapping Mrs. Wolf's packages."

As Lanna hurried off to her next shopping errand, other customers piled in. They all had that hungry look, since Christmas was a handful of days away. Cole frowned, debating. "It's getting busy. I don't want to miss an opportunity for a sale. I should stay. Maybe—"

"No," Eberta scolded him, shaking her head. "I know it's a good time for business, but if you don't meet that lady at the train, what will she think? It will make a bad impression."

"This is a marriage of convenience." He'd been clear about that in his advertisement and in the many letters he'd exchanged with Mrs. Mercy Jacobs. "She's hardly expecting a bouquet and courting words. She'd likely appreciate a friendly greeting. Perhaps you could do it."

"Pa." Amelia stepped in, rolling her eyes and shaking her head at him as if she wasn't surprised by this at all. "For once, leave the shop to Eberta. This is really important."

It wasn't the shop he cared about as much as the fact that he wasn't so good at relationships. On this side of the counter, he understood his role. He felt comfortable with it. Greeting customers, totaling up purchases, helping people find what they were looking for. This was a transaction he understood.

His true worry that he would disappoint Mercy Jacobs, the woman who'd traveled so far with the heartfelt promise to love his daughter. What if she was secretly hoping for some semblance of a real marriage? What if she'd been wishing for a man capable of loving her?

His heart had been broken so long ago, and he couldn't even remember when it had been whole.

A whistle sounded in the distance, faint through the walls of the shop.

"It's coming! We need to hurry." Amelia's much smaller hand crept into his. "Oh, I can't wait to meet my new mother."

She held on so tight, the way she used to do when she was small.

It was a reminder that she was still a little girl, that while she'd grown tall and slender, she absolutely needed the woman who would be getting off that train.

"Angel Falls, next stop!" The conductor's friendly voice boomed through the car.

A frantic flutter of heartbeats tapped against her sternum. Mercy drew in a slow breath, trying to steady her nerves. This was the moment of truth. When she discovered whether everything Cole Matheson had written about his town, his daughter and himself were true. Her palms went clammy as she worried for her son. How would George feel if Mr. Matheson wasn't the man he claimed to be?

She smoothed down the boy's flyaway cowlick, willing it to stay down for a good first impression.

Just trust in the Lord, she told herself. *Trust the feelings and the signs that have brought you here.*

"Look, Ma!" George went up on both knees, struggling to get a good view as the train started its slow descent on the town. "There's horses in that field. *Horses.*"

"So I see." She leaned in, love in her heart for her son, daring to hope for him. "Look at them run."

"They're racin' the train. Wow." George pressed his nose against the glass, hungry to lap up the sight of the majestic creatures in shades of blacks and browns galloping against the snowy-white world. His boyish shoulders lifted up with satisfaction. "What if those are Mr. Matheson's horses? What if one of 'em will be mine?"

"That would be nice, wouldn't it?" She let her son dream, her sweet good boy, giving thanks for the man who'd promised to give George one of his horses and riding lessons. Everything George had been dreaming. Her throat closed up tight. She needed to believe Cole was a man who kept his promises. Her late husband, Timothy, had meant well, but he hadn't been so good with that. She hoped history wasn't about to repeat itself.

A touch on her sleeve caught her attention. The conductor stood there, smiling down at her, his gray hair peeking out from beneath his cap. "I'll get your satchels for you, ma'am. You have your attention full with your fine son."

"I'm gonna learn to ride like a real cowboy." George beamed, his grin ear to ear, his button face flushed pink with pleasure. Why, she'd never seen his navy blue eyes so bright.

She didn't know what she'd do if Cole Matheson let him down. Tears burned behind her eyes at the thought and she smiled weakly up at the conductor. "Thank you, Mr. Blake."

"My pleasure." The kindly man set both her and George's satchels on the floor at her feet. "I see you're wearing your mistletoe."

"I pinned it on. I need all the help I can get." She tried to laugh to hide her reservations, but she feared she didn't quite succeed.

Something that looked like understanding flashed in the older man's eyes. The anxious flutter in her chest doubled. So much depended on this first meeting. She thanked the conductor, who moved along to help another passenger with her bags, and looked out the window with George.

It does look like a friendly town, she thought over the squealing sound of the brakes. She drank in the sight of tidy streets, the white steeple of a church spearing up over the storefronts and the school bell tower not far away. The train made a final jerk to a stop, and the depot's platform stretched out before them. A half-dozen people waited for the train, searching the windows anxiously as if eager to be reunited with loved ones—all except for one man.

He was brawny, muscled and tall. His black Stetson tilted to cover half of his face. What she could see was his strong, square jaw, a chiseled mouth that naturally drew into a straight, stern line, and a dimple carved into an angled chin. This man stood apart from the others, staring at the plank boards in front of his black cowboy boots. Maybe in his mid-thirties, she guessed. He wore denims, a black duster and a look of resignation.

As if he felt her scrutiny, he lifted his head higher, knuckled back the brim of his hat to reveal a granite face, high cheekbones and startling blue eyes. Across the distance, their gazes met and she felt the shock of it strike through her like a lightning bolt. All the way to her soul.

Cole Matheson, she thought, beyond all doubt. And by the look of him, he really was a cowboy. All he was missing were spurs.

That was a good sign, right? He hadn't exaggerated that piece, anyway. Hopes for her son broke loose and she smiled, truly smiled.

Maybe it was another sign—and not a good one—that Cole Matheson didn't smile back.

Chapter Two

"Pa! Do you see her?" Amelia bounded ahead of him, skirts and wild strawberry hair batted by the icy wind.

"Yes, I see her." He swallowed hard against a thickness in his throat, surprised to hear his voice strained and not sounding at all like his own. Through the glazed glass, the prim-and-proper lady was shadowed, hardly more than an outline of a colorful hat and the delicate curve of cheek and chin. Eyes too far away to see the color through the glass fastened on his, and he felt the plea and worries as if they were his own. As hard as this was for him, he thought with a sigh, it had to be the same for her.

This was the moment of truth. Resigned and grim, he squared his shoulders and marched forward like a dutiful soldier. He was about to find out if this mail-order marriage idea was a mistake or a solution.

"Oh, she's pretty. That *has* to be her." Amelia glanced over her shoulder to throw him a happy look. Sparkles gleamed in her blue eyes; the wind's bite and joy turned her dear face pink. "She's wearing the brown hat with the purple flower like she said she would, and look at the boy with her. He's blond. That's George."

George. Something hollow twisted in Cole's chest, in a place that had been empty for so long. Eagerness he hadn't felt in aeons surged through him and he turned his attention to the child. Round face, a tumble of blond hair, big worried eyes. Then the boy was gone, disappeared from the window. Cole froze in place, not wanting to move forward in enthusiasm the way Amelia was, needing to be reserved. He needed that shield, that protection.

"Mrs. Mercy!" Amelia rushed toward the passengers disembarking, her shoes pounding against the planks of the platform. Most unladylike, but he didn't raise his voice to rein her in. That would mean he would have to move closer, draw attention to himself and make the elegant, willowy woman easing down the steps glance his way.

She was beautiful. Really beautiful. His jaw dropped in disbelief. His pulse screeched to a stop. Surprised, he could only stare at the unexpected loveliness of her face, her carefully carved, china-doll features, porcelain skin, graceful sloping nose and lustrous blue eyes that made every person on the platform turn and stare at her. He couldn't look away. Why on earth did she need to be a mail-order bride?

The woman spotted Amelia, and a caring smile transformed her reserved beauty into sheer loveliness radiating such warmth it made his throat close up entirely. This lady was kind, kinder than he'd ever dared to imagine, he thought as she took her son by the hand and helped him make the leap off the lower step and onto the board platform.

How could this be? he wondered. How could this lady be everything he'd wanted for Amelia? A man like him didn't get that lucky, and he'd given up looking for blessings a long time ago. God had forgotten about him an hour after his stepfather had married his widowed mother. But Amelia… The Lord hadn't forgotten Amelia. That was all that mattered.

"Or can I call you Ma?" Amelia gushed, wrapped her arms around Mercy Jacobs as if she'd known her forever. She bounced back and boldly grabbed hold of both Mercy's satchels. The girl's shoulders sank from the weight of the heavy bags, but she refused to let go.

"Ma?" Mercy's forehead crinkled, her soft mouth tilting upward. "It's not official yet. Should the wedding come first?"

"I don't care. You're *going* to get married. Maybe that's not what you want me to call you, but I've been practicing. Mrs. Mercy is probably best, that's what Pa says I should call you, because Mrs. Jacobs is too formal, like I don't know you at all, but I really know you because of the two letters so we aren't *complete* strangers."

"You may call me whatever you like, dear girl." To her credit, Mercy Jacobs bit her bottom lip to keep from laughing. Her expressive dark blue eyes telegraphed caring, as if she'd already fallen in love with the child. "But I don't want you to feel as if I'm replacing your mother."

"Oh, I hardly remember her, not that I don't love her, too, but I want to call you Ma." Amelia looked as if she were about to float away with pure joy at any minute. "I want you for a mother so much."

"Just the way I want you, Amelia." Warmth. Gentleness. The kind that only a mother could bring. That's what he saw as Mercy Jacobs gently brushed strawberry-blond tangles out of Amelia's eyes. "I've always wanted a daughter, too. Something tells me I couldn't have found a better one if I'd looked all over the world."

Overcome, Amelia fell silent, tears standing in her eyes.

George watched the woman and girl curiously, standing back from his mother, obviously a shy boy. Quiet.

Just like Cole had been at that age. Still was, if truth be told. He didn't like emotions, did his best to avoid them—he squared his shoulders, wrangling down every last one. He watched Mercy Jacobs introduce her son to Amelia, who greeted him with enthusiasm. She thought she might like having a brother, the girl explained, as her best friends were boys. Did George know how to sled?

The boy shook his head and cautiously took his mother's hand.

"I'll teach you," Amelia promised.

Cole winced, wondering what refined Mercy Jacobs might be thinking of that. Determined to protect his daughter and to keep her from seeming unladylike, which she was and which he had to believe Mercy could change, he bolted forward.

"Cole." Mercy faced him, fastening the power of her unguarded gaze on him.

He stumbled. He'd never seen anything as genuine and sincere as the hope and silent plea in those navy blue depths. Feeling inadequate, he extended his hand. "Mrs. Jacobs."

Maybe it was too formal. She seemed surprised for a moment. She squared her slender shoulders, a little bit guarded, and reserve crept into her gaze. As if he wasn't meeting expectations.

He winced, as she wouldn't be the first woman to size him up and react the same. He cleared his throat, attempting to sound hospitable. "Nice to finally meet you."

"It is." She looked a little nervous, just as he was, and faced him directly. "I have to say the town is charming, and as for Amelia, well, she's obviously everything you said she was."

"Beware, I may have left out a few key pieces of information about my daughter." He shrugged, feeling more awkward than he could remember being in a long while. "Just thought I should warn you."

"Pa! I can't believe you said that." Amelia whirled to face Mercy. "Really, Pa has this old-fashioned notion that girls can't do anything that boys can do."

"I didn't say that you can't. Only that you shouldn't," he corrected.

"I think this is going to be interesting." Holding her son's hand in hers, Mercy smiled. She extended her free arm to his daughter and drew her in against her side, as warmly as her real mother should have done.

Amelia beamed, gazing up at Mercy Jacobs as if she'd hung the moon and all the stars.

This was so much more than he'd ever hoped for. The woman was not only caring, but just as prim and proper as he'd deduced from her letters. Her blond hair was tucked up behind her brown hat, every strand in perfect place. Her brown wool coat, while showing a lot of wear, was in good repair, buttoned to her throat. The toes of her polished albeit patched shoes peeked from beneath her skirt ruffle. But it was her face that told him the most about her, the wholesome goodness shining from her, the cautious set of her mouth, the demure way she lowered her gaze from his. The concern she showed for her son, the caring she extended to Amelia.

A lump rose in his throat, and he was ashamed of giving in to his feelings. It was simply too much to bear. Mercy Jacobs had lived up to her word.

Now it was his turn to live up to his.

"Hello, George." He knelt down so he was eye to eye with the quiet boy who'd been studying him beneath the brim of his cap. Cole held out one gloved hand. "I've been looking forward to meeting you since the first time your mother wrote me about you."

"You have?" The boy gulped, surprise and hope flashing in his eyes. Shy, the boy blushed, searching for words, perhaps not knowing what to say next.

Cole sympathized with the kid. He knew what it was like to be without a father. He knew what it felt like to look at a man and wish more than anything he could be the father you needed. With a grimace, Cole closed the door on his memories, the ones from after his mother's marriage, of the disillusionment and fear he'd felt at the hands of his stepfather. He choked up, vowing little George would never know such things.

"I've wanted a son all this time," he told the boy. "I work long hours in my store so I don't have as much time as I want to ride my horses. If I teach you to ride, like I promised, will you help me out by riding them for me?"

"Uh-huh." George vigorously nodded his head, a world of hope filling him up, showing his dreams.

"Good." Cole had dreams, too, ones he'd been trying to hold back. He loved his daughter with all he had, but he'd wanted a bigger family. Daughters to protect and care for, sons to teach and share his love of horses and inherit his store. Not knowing how to say these things, he reached out and gripped the boy's shoulder. The childish feel of him, small and vulnerable, filled Cole's heart. Just filled it.

Good to know at least there was room for dreams to come true, even at this time in a man's life.

"C'mon," he said to the child, holding out his hand. "Let's get you out of this cold. Look, it's starting to snow."

"It's real snowy here." George let go of his mother, gazing up at her as if to ask permission.

"Stay where I can see you." She nodded. "Don't run ahead."

"I won't," he said, puffing out his chest. "I'll stay right beside my new pa."

George placed his hand in the man's much larger, stronger one. Seeing those capable fingers enclose around her son's gave her the courage to let him trail ahead of her. It wasn't easy letting go, trusting a man she didn't know well with her son's heart. But Cole seemed to take the responsibility seriously as he led the boy across the platform.

"You have to see the place we fixed up for you." Amelia surged ahead, holding on tight. "There are rooms Pa rents above the store, but he kept one for you and George. Temporarily, until you get married. It's got everything you'll need in it. Me and Eberta, she works for Pa in the store, we got the prettiest things we could find."

"That sounds wonderful. I can't tell you what that means." She tapped down the stairs, checking on George's progress. Already he was tripping along the boardwalk alongside Cole while tiny airy snowflakes danced in the air around him. She turned back to the girl, her soon-to-be daughter, and drank in all her wonderfulness. Strawberry-blond hair, enthusiastic blue eyes, a faint trace of freckles across her nose. Her zest for life was refreshing. "I'm so happy to be here with you, Amelia."

"I know! That's just how I feel, too." The girl's grip tightened, as if she never intended to let go.

Affection welled up, unexpected and instant. Just like that, she felt a mother's bond to this child. As if God had meant for them to be together, as if He'd sat in His kingdom knitting their kindred hearts together. Gratitude filled her as she headed down the boardwalk, making her eyes blur.

"That's the post office right there." Amelia pointed across the tidy street. Snow was shoveled into piles against the base of the boardwalk, keeping the way clear for shoppers. A horse and wagon rolled by with a rattle. “There’s the milliner’s shop.”

Mercy blinked against the grateful tears, bringing the town into focus. Colorful awnings protected the boardwalk from the snow, cheerful front display windows advertised presents and Christmas decorations adorned front doors and hitching posts. Garlands and wreaths and Christmas trees lit by tiny little candles.

The snow fell harder now, driven by a brisk wind. It clouded her view of George ahead, casting him in silhouette. Little boy, hand in hand with a big man. His new pa. Gratitude rushed up so strongly, her eyes blurred again.

Be everything you promised to my son, she asked, watching the faint, impressive line of Cole’s broad shoulders. *Please.*

“There’s Grummel’s Barber Shop.” Amelia danced ahead, pointing across the street. “Right next to Lawson’s Mercantile. We get our groceries there. Oh, and this is our store.”

“Matheson’s Dry Goods.” Mercy tilted her head back to read the sign swinging in the wind. Icy flecks of snow tapped her face as she squinted at the long bank of front windows belonging to the shop.

My, she’d never expected a man who advertised for a mail-order wife to be prosperous. Her jaw dropped at the size of the building, at the tasteful displays of fine products behind the glass and the expansive, impressive oak counter spanning two sides inside the store. A merry bell jangled as Cole opened the door.

"Eberta and I decorated the windows. Didn't we do a good job?" Amelia tugged her across the threshold, through the door Cole held for them.

"Yes, it's lovely. I love the way you decorated the Christmas tree." She breezed past him, aware of him watching her carefully, aware of a sort of sparkle in her heart as their sleeves brushed. Just for a moment, just for an instant, and it was gone. She stumbled after Amelia, breathless, not sure at all what had happened.

"You must be Mercy." A kindly plump woman circled around the counter, her salt-and-pepper hair tied sternly back into a strict, no-nonsense bun. She wore a brown dress with no adornment, but a friendly smile chased away any impression of sternness. "I can't tell you how good it is to meet you. This has been a long time coming in my opinion. If there's anything this one needs, it's a mother's guiding hand."

"I'm not sure how guiding I'll be, but I'll do my best." Mercy took the woman's offered hand, squeezing it warmly. When she looked into those dark eyes, she saw a friend. "You must be Eberta."

"Yes, and no matter what that man tells you, I am more than capable of running this store without him." The elder woman arranged her pleasant face into a schoolmarm's glare. "Yes, very capable indeed. Cole, what are you doing back so soon? I thought you were taking the rest of the day off."

"There's thirty or so more minutes left of the business day." Cole closed the door with a jangle of the overhead bell, swiping snow off his hat. "It is the busy season."

His casual shrug belied his true feelings, or so Mercy suspected. She untied her hat, snow sifting to the floor, watching the man. Here, in the lamplight, she could see things she hadn't been able to spot in the shadowy gloam outside. The deep lines radiating from his eyes, the sadness in them, the air about him as if he'd given up on hope entirely.

She recalled what he'd written in his letters. He'd told her his heart had been broken long ago. He had only pieces of it left to give, but he would give what he had to George.

She'd taken that to mean there were no pieces left over for her. And that was fine. George was what mattered here. She wasn't exactly sure why that made her sad.

"That man, it's all about work with him." Eberta waved her hand, dismissing him, in the way of a good friend. Caring warmed her voice, softened the scowl she sent him. "We'll see if you can change that, Mercy. In my opinion, it would be an improvement."

"So you're telling me this man needs to change for the better?" She couldn't help teasing, keeping her tone gentle and soft, so that perhaps he would understand. "I suppose that's true of every man, but I've vowed to accept Cole as he is."

"Bad decision," Eberta quipped, bustling back behind the counter when a customer approached. "Don't you think, Mrs. Frost?"

"Absolutely." A lovely blonde lady nodded emphatically as she set her purchases on the counter. "Goodness, my Sam was a disaster when I first met him. He took a lot of training up."

"Funny." Cole's face heated, turning bright red. "I seem to remember Sam was just fine to begin with."

"A man *would* say that," Mrs. Frost teased as she pulled several dollar bills from her reticule. She rolled her eyes, good-naturedly. "If only they could see themselves from a woman's perspective. Mercy, is it? I'm Molly. So glad to meet you. Something tells me you are exactly what a certain someone needs."

"Hey, you can say my name," Amelia spoke up sweetly. "It doesn't hurt my feelings. I know I'm incorrigible. Pa tells me all the time."

"Incorrigible?" Mercy noticed the way Cole winced, and also the fond look the customer, Mrs. Frost, sent the girl. She liked the sense of community here. She liked the friendliness these people had for one another. It chased away more of her anxieties. Whatever was ahead, Cole was clearly a man others thought well of. She winked at Amelia. "No one mentioned incorrigible in their letters."

"I did warn you there would be surprises." Cole looked terribly uncomfortable as he shrugged off his wool, tailored coat. His green flannel shirt looked to be new, of high quality, fitted well to his muscled shoulders and granite chest. "Molly, perhaps it would be best not to point this out until after the wedding?"

"Right, what was I thinking?" Molly winked, accepted her change from Eberta and her packages. "Mercy, it's lovely to meet you. I hope to see you again soon. Amelia, try and stay out of trouble."

"I'm never in trouble." Amelia grinned widely. "It all depends on how you look at it."

"Hmm, you sound like my girls." Molly laughed, smiled warmly at Mercy as she passed and leaned in to say something quietly to Cole. She waved at George, slipped through the door Cole opened for her and was gone, leaving them alone.

Even in the busy store full of bustling shoppers, even with their children between them, she felt alone. Lonely. Mercy sighed quietly, for this was what she had expected. It was what she knew, what her first marriage had become. Why would this relationship be any different? As if not knowing what to say, either, Cole turned to help George off with his coat, for one of his buttons had gotten stuck. She'd sewn it on too tightly when it had popped off on the train.

"Amelia," Cole said as he worked the button free. "Why don't you take Mercy and George to their rooms? That is, unless you want to stay here and help me in the store, George."

George bit his bottom lip, debating. Torn between going with his mother or staying with his new father-to-be. His blue eyes met hers imploring. "Can I stay here, Ma?"

"Of course you can. You come upstairs and find me when you're ready." Her words felt scratchy, sounded thick and raw with the emotion she felt. A mix of gratitude and relief and sadness. In gaining this marriage, she had to let go of George just a little bit, to share him with Cole.

This was for the best, she hold herself, knowing deep in her stomach it was true. Look at the care the man took with her son. Leading him around the counter, talking to him kindly, telling the boy he was just the helper he needed. Dreams for her son, the ones that had brought her here, filled her heart. George gazed up at the man with adoration, eyes wide with wonder.

Yes, a loveless marriage was worth that, she thought to buoy herself, letting Amelia pull her away. She touched her fingertips to the sprig of mistletoe pinned to her coat collar, remembering the conductor's kindness. Well, she did not need a kiss on Christmas. No, she wanted a happy son and a happy daughter. It was the children who mattered.

Chapter Three

"It's getting dark." Amelia dropped both satchels on the landing outside the door at the top of the narrow staircase, turned the knob and burst across the threshold. Her shoes tapped a merry rhythm as she darted ahead into the twilight room. "But Eberta lit the fire for you. It's toasty warm up here."

"Yes, it is." Mercy unbuttoned her coat, moving into the shadowed rooms. Her steps echoed around her. "Can I help?"

"No, I've got it." A flame snapped to life and Amelia carefully lit a glass lamp on a table next to a horsehair sofa. A nice, comfortable-looking sofa. The girl carried the match to the second lamp on an identical table, careful to protect the flame. "What do you think? Eberta and I worked real hard."

"You surely did. It's wonderful, Amelia." Her throat ached at the thoughtfulness. What a comfortable room. A warm wool afghan graced the back of the sofa, quilted throw pillows added color to the room and lacy doilies lent an air of elegance. Warm braided rugs made the space cozy. “Thank you. I’ve never felt more at home.”

“Eberta made all of the afghans and lacy things.” Amelia lit the second lamp, shaking out the match.

Light danced to life, flickering into the recesses of the room, showing off a small kitchen and an eating area in the corner. A doorway must lead to the bedroom. After such a long journey, sleeping on the train, the thought of a warm comfortable bed made her weak in the knees. She eased onto the edge of the sofa, hand to her heart, more thankful than words could say.

“I think Eberta was hoping I’d take a notion to try the needle arts,” Amelia explained as she grabbed a pot holder and opened the potbellied stove’s door. Reddish-orange flames raged inside the metal belly. “Nope, there’s plenty of fuel. You know, I have no interest in learning to knit and stuff, but Pa says I have to learn. I suppose it would be okay if you taught me, but I want you to know my feelings.”

“I hear you loud and clear.” Mercy reached out to smooth a stray strawberry-blond lock of the girl’s hair. What a sparkle she was, full of life and light. “It might be a nice way for you and me to get to know each other. My ma and I would sit for hours on a Sunday afternoon knitting or sewing away, just talking.”

"What was your ma like?" Amelia tilted her head to one side, curious. "Was she like you?"

"Goodness, no. She was very refined. Very cultured. She was the youngest daughter of a very wealthy man and ran away from home to marry someone her family didn't approve of. She became a farmer's wife, but she never regretted it. She said love was the greatest treasure in this life."

"Pa says children are." Amelia grinned, full of mischief. "Except for me. He says I'm nothing but trouble."

"Is that so? I'm dying to know what kind of trouble you are." While she waited for the girl's answer, the motherly side of her couldn't help wondering about George. Or the man with him, the tall and tough-looking store owner. Was that the rumble of Cole's baritone through the floorboards? And why was she straining to listen?

"Well, you know about the sledding." Amelia scrunched up her face, most adorably. She rolled her gaze toward the ceiling, thinking. "I tend to get in trouble at school for whispering or writing notes to my friends on my slate."

"I have a hard time imagining that," Mercy gently teased.

"I know! I try to be good, I really do, but I'm naturally bubbly." Amelia didn't seem all that troubled by it. "I have snowball making down to a fine art. No one can make a better one than me. The trick is to spit on it just a little. It ices up, so it holds together better when you throw it."

"Good to know." Mercy wondered just exactly what kind of influence Amelia might be on poor George. An aspect she hadn't considered when she'd been in North Carolina, trying to decide which newspaper advertisement to answer.

A tap of footsteps caught her attention. A floorboard squeaked as a man's heavy gait marched closer, accompanied by the patter of a boy's. Her attention leaped, eager to gaze upon her son and see how he was doing, but her senses seemed focused on the tall, shadowed man pausing outside the open door to grip the fallen satchels.

Oh, my. His thick dark hair swirled in a thick whirl around his crown and fell to his collar. As he straightened, hauling the satchels with him, muscles bunched and played beneath the material of his shirt. He strode powerfully into the room like a man more suited to the wild outdoors, hefting a rifle at a bear, perhaps. He dominated the room and made her pulse skid to a stop. He looked immense with his broad shoulders and muscled girth. When he caught her watching him, he jerked his gaze away, staring hard at the floor.

"I'll put these in the bedroom." The smoky pitch of his tone came gruff and distant. As if he didn't want to talk to her. He said nothing more, crossing behind the couch, where she couldn't see him, where his step drummed in the room like a hollow heartbeat. “George, did you want to come along?”

“Yes, sir!” The boy hurried after him, disappearing into the shadowed, narrow hallway.

Mercy didn’t know why her chest ached so much it hurt to breathe. Her husband-to-be was doing his best to avoid her. He was courteous and responsible toward her, but she felt a vast distance settling between them. It felt lonely.

“Pa?” Amelia hopped to her feet with a flat-footed thud. “What about supper? We are gonna have Ma and George over, right?”

“She’s not your ma yet.” His voice thundered from the far room, sounding muffled and irritated. Something landed on the floor. Likely the satchels. “It’ll be best to let Mercy and George settle into their rooms. They’ve traveled a long way. They must be tired, right, George?”

“Sorta.” The boy’s thin response sounded uncertain. “I was kinda hopin’ to see your horses.”

“I have tomorrow set aside for that.” Cole’s tone warmed and he strode into sight with the child at his side. What an image they made. Towering man, little boy. “You want to be rested up because it’ll be a big day. A good day, I promise you that. Besides, I’m going to bed early to be set and ready to go come morning.”

“Then I will be, too.” George nodded, his face

scrunching up determinedly. "Will I really get to ride tomorrow?"

"My word of honor." Cole ran his big hand lightly over the top of the boy's head, a fatherly gesture. "But there's more to riding horses. You also have to learn how to take care of them."

"I know. I'm good at sweeping the steps whenever Ma tells me to. That's sorta like cleaning a barn. Do I get my own pitchfork?"

"I got one especially for you. I'll teach you everything you need to know." Cole stepped away, and for an instant a father's longing flashed across his face. When he glanced her way, the look had vanished. He squared his shoulders, his reserve going up. "Eberta is finishing with the last customer downstairs. When she's done, she'll head over to the diner next door. Amelia's going with her. George can go, too, if you wish. They can fetch your meals, while you and I talk."

Talk. Her chest tensed up so tightly her ribs felt ready to crack. "I suppose that sounds like a wise plan."

"Good." Cole nodded in his daughter's direction before turning to warm his hands at the stove.

"C'mon, George. Let's go." Amelia hopped forward, skirts swishing, and held out her hand. "The diner has the best cookies. If Eberta is in a good mood, and something tells me that she might be, we can talk her into getting us dessert."

George quietly took the girl's hand, hesitating to glance across the room. Mercy recognized his worried look, so she nodded reassuringly, letting him know it would be all right.

"I'll be right here waiting for you," she told him, her good boy. He blew out a breath, perhaps shrugging off his anxiety, and took Amelia's hand. The two trotted off, Amelia chattering away, as if determined to make them friends.

The room felt lonelier without the children in it, with only the two of them and their marriage agreement. Mercy's palms grew damp as the silence stretched. She didn't know if she should stand up and join Cole at the stove or continue to wait for him to speak. Since she wasn't a meek woman, she scooted farther up on the cushion, poised on the edge of it and studied the man with his back to her, rigid as stone.

This wasn't easy for him, either. That realization made it easier to break the silence.

"George already adores you." She folded her hands together, lacing her fingers, staring at her work-roughened hands. "Thank you for being so welcoming to him, for being everything you promised in your letters."

"Why wouldn't I keep my word?" His tense back went rigid. His wide shoulders bunched. Then he blew out an audible huff of breath. "We agreed to be honest with one another."

"We did." She could sense an old hurt in the air,

maybe something from his marriage. Heaven knew she had issues from hers. "Amelia is delightful. Everything I knew she would be."

"Even rambunctious?" A slight dollop of humor chased the chill from his words.

"I suspected from her letters that she had a zest for life." Slowly, she stood. Uncertain, she bit her bottom lip, wanting to reach out to the man, to her husband-to-be. "I was less certain what you would be like from your letters, although I read so many of them."

"Likely I disappoint." More of that humor and something else, something that seemed to make the shadows in the room darken, creeping ever closer.

"No, I may be the disappointment." She brushed at a wrinkle in her wool dress, hoping he hadn't noticed the fraying hem she hadn't been able to mend on the train. "I wasn't prepared for you to be so prosperous. And, well, I'm—"

"Just what Amelia needs," he interrupted firmly, turning to face her. Resolute, confident, certain. Muscles jumped along his set jaw. "I learned a lot about you from your letters. You are honest and loyal—you worked hard for your son. You are unselfish enough to endure a marriage to a stranger for his sake."

"Endure?" Her voice wobbled, betraying her, letting him know how difficult this really was. "That rather sounds like a jail sentence."

"I didn't mean it to be." Part quip, part serious. Sadness eked into his gaze, darkening his eyes to a night blue, as if all the light had drained from the room. He shrugged one capable shoulder. "Maybe we can come to an agreement so we both won't be disappointed. Rules to live by, that type of thing. We're going to be bound together in this life. Don't know why we can't make it tolerable."

"Gee, now I'm really excited about marrying you." She smiled, and her gentle teasing softened the stony cast to his face. He broke into a half smile, and the lean planes of his cheeks creased into manly crinkles. He had dimples. Who knew? Mercy grinned back, feeling a little fluttery. Not only did her new fiancé have dimples, but he was handsome.

Very, very handsome.

"That's what I want to talk to you about." He raked one hand through his thick, dark hair. "I know we wrote about a simple wedding. Just the four of us in front of the minister the day after you arrived."

"Seeing this room set up so comfortably…" She gestured at the nice sofa and matching overstuffed chair, the small drop-leaf end table set up with two chairs near the kitchen area window. "It's obvious you want to postpone the wedding."

"For Amelia's sake." He blew out another sigh, looking tense again. "I didn't think to tell her what we agreed to. Something simple, quick, no fuss. But the problem with that is it sets a bad example of what marriage ought to be. This between us is—"

"A sensible arrangement," she finished for him, seeing how hard this was for him to talk about. It was hard for her, too, remembering the young bride she'd been when she'd married Timothy, so full of hopes and joy she'd practically floated down the church aisle. "You want her to keep her illusions of marriage. You want to protect her."

"So, you do understand." Relief stood out starkly on his face, carving into the grooved lines bracketing his mouth. He folded his big, six-foot frame into the chair. "I didn't realize she had her heart set on a proper ceremony with a new dress and family and friends attending. Not until I spotted this."

He reached for a child's school slate set aside on an end table. "Amelia has been dying to show you her plans."

"For a real wedding?" Mercy's hand trembled as she reached for the slate. She had to lean in to grab the wooden frame, close enough to feel the fan of his breath against her cheek. She breathed in the pleasant scent of clean male, winter wind and soap.

Little flutters settled in her stomach again, which was strange. Surely she wasn't attracted to him. She bit her bottom lip, uncertain what to think. Perhaps she'd simply gone too long between meals. Heart pounding, she eased onto the sofa cushion, taking in the girl's wedding plans, written out in a careful, cheerful script on the slate's black background.

Her heart dropped at the list. *To do:* Amelia had written. *Invite everyone. Flowers for the bride. Candles for the church. The dress in Cora's shop window, the one with the lace and velvet for my new ma. A big cake for the celebration. A Christmas Eve wedding.* Beside the last item, Amelia had drawn a little heart.

"She has her hopes set higher than I realized," Cole said quietly, the deep timbre of his voice rolling over Mercy like a touch, as if imploring her to understand. "I know we agreed on a simple ceremony. You said that was what you wanted. No fuss, no pretense."

"But this way, with your friends as witnesses." Mercy's fingertip hovered over the words Amelia had written, over the plans she'd made. Her chest ached, torn between the old and the new. "What will they think?"

"It doesn't matter. I'm not a man given to pretense. They knew the truth, Mercy. This is an agreement, simple as that." He swallowed hard, as if he were troubled, too, perhaps plagued with memories like she was, of a love that was gone for good. Burying a spouse was a sorrow that lasted. He shot to his feet, pacing to the window. "I understand if you'd rather keep to our arrangement."

"I never expected to walk down the aisle again."

Carefully she set the slate aside. Everything inside of her began to spin. Her thoughts. Her hopes. What she'd resigned her life to be. "I never thought such a bright spot could come my way. I really adore your daughter, Cole. I don't want to disappoint her."

"Neither do I." He turned from the window, grateful. "We do this for the children?"

"For the children." The agreement stood between them, precious and unyielding, the one thing they had in common. When he managed to smile at her with his lopsided half grin that was sad at the same time, she smiled back. The distance between them didn't feel as enormous.

Or as lonely.

"Thank you, Mercy." The muscle twisted in his jaw, harder this time, giving her a hint of how hard this must be for him.

What had he gone through? she wondered. His loss was as great as hers. She knew what walking the road of grief as a surviving spouse and parent felt like. For the first time she could see—truly see—that the things she'd prayed for when she'd read his letters and wrote to him in turn could come to pass. They could do this, make things good between them. Two strangers knitting their lives together. "I should be the one thanking you. These rooms are homey."

"Good, that's how I want you to feel—at home." His one-sided grin returned and he jammed his hands into his denim pockets. "Eberta and Amelia robbed our house to make you comfortable here. I didn't object."

"This is from your home?"

"*Our* home," he corrected.

"But what are you and Amelia sitting on?"

"We have some furniture left, don't worry." He glanced out the window, squinting down at the dark street keeping a sharp eye out for the kids. He liked that she was concerned. Yes, she was everything he'd hoped for. A widow, who'd lost her heart, too. Kindly, for Amelia's sake. Proper and soft-spoken, the way he wanted Amelia to be. This might just work out all right.

Relieved, he watched the snow fall. When he caught sight of George hopping out of the diner and onto the boardwalk, the hard tangle of emotions eased. Yes, this was a rare blessing. Not that he believed God even remembered him these days, but surely the Lord watched over the children. He reached for the curtain ties and let the fabric fall over the dark glass and lacy sheers. "We have a few more minutes to ourselves. I want to talk about those rules."

"Rules." She brushed a few stray blond curls out of her face, silken soft wisps that had escaped her simple, braided bun. "What did you have in mind?"

"First off, I want to agree not to talk about the past." He felt as if he was suffocating just thinking of it. Those dark times were better off behind him. "And I expect you to live on a budget."

She didn't bat an eye. Perhaps some women in this situation would be outraged, others defensive. Mercy sat spine straight, delicate jaw set, not even mildly surprised. "I'm a widow supporting a son. I'm excellent with budgets. I'll expect you to stay on the budget, too. No reckless spending."

"Agreed." There he went, smiling again. This woman had an effect on him. He hadn't expected to actually like her. He pushed away from the window. "I want my house clean and meals on time. I like order."

"I see." She bit her bottom lip, as if holding back laughter.

What did he say that was so funny? He circled around to sit back down in the chair, facing her. Amusement glinted in her eyes, so blue they took his breath away. The color reminded him of summer night skies and summer breezes. His breathing hitched, startling him. It wasn't like him to think this way. He wasn't a man given to whimsy. "Am I amusing you?"

"Yes." Her smile could light up a room. Sweetness beamed from her like golden rays slanting down through the clouds from the heavens. She tilted her head to one side, the lamplight finding her, burnishing her hair, caressing her soft cheek. "I have some rules for you, too."

"I suppose that's only fair."

"You may tell me what to do only two times a day." She arched a slender eyebrow at him in a gentle challenge.

"Only twice?" he inquired, curious, grinning against his will.

"Keep in mind I may not oblige you." She folded her hands neatly in her lap, just sheer loveliness. Her heart-shaped face was guileless and unguarded. Anyone just looking at her could see she didn't have a mean bone in her body.

Whoever her husband had been, he'd been a blessed man, Cole thought. He was more than thankful to have her as Amelia's mother and his helpmate.

"All right," he agreed. "We'll not boss each other around."

"Agreed. I'll not say an unkind thing to you ever, if you do me the same courtesy." Her chin hiked up a notch, a delicate show of strength. Something sad flashed in her eyes so briefly he barely noticed it. He opened his mouth to ask about it, but then remembered his own rule. Keep the past in the past. And he shut his mouth with a click of his teeth.

Not your business, he reminded himself. Knowing about her and what she'd been through would only soften his defenses, and he didn't want to like her. He didn't want to care. It was best for all around if they kept this strictly a convenient arrangement.

The door swung open, hitting the wall like a gunshot. His daughter sashayed in, balancing a wrapped meal in both hands, practically skipping. Her skirts swirled around her, and her smile was so big it was all he could see.

"We got you a real good supper, Mercy." Amelia beamed her full-strength charm Mercy's way. "George told me your favorite, and so that's what we ordered. We even got you lots of cookies, too. George said that's his favorite."

"Yep, it sure is," the kid confirmed with a nod, tromping through the doorway and into the room, cheeks pink, dusted with snow, cute in that way of small boys.

Cole's chest tightened, aching with hope. It was going to be nice having a son. In all honesty, he'd found a good one. He cleared his throat, hoping he didn't sound gruff when he spoke.

"You and your ma have a nice meal, settle in and have a good night." He almost reached out to the boy, to tousle the kid's hair, but something held him back. Maybe it was the ache dead center in his chest, the one that hurt like hope coming to life, as if a frozen part of his heart was starting to awaken. But that couldn't be right. Too many pieces were gone for good. So he didn't know why it hurt, why he felt overwhelmed as he nodded to Eberta, who was carrying the other meal into the room.

He knew only that it was time to leave before the pain became too much and he stopped breathing entirely. "I reckon a soft bed will be a welcome thing after sleeping on the train."

"More than you know." Mercy took a step toward him, her dark blue eyes radiating a quiet communication.

He nodded, sensing her thankfulness, understanding what she could not say. It was how he felt, too. He crossed the threshold, heading down the stairs, calling for his daughter to follow.

Chapter Four

All through the night, he was plagued by dreams of a golden-haired lady with a silent hope in the midnight-blue depths of her eyes. Cole woke the next morning to the silence that came after a great storm. He stared at the shadowy ceiling in the early morning's darkness and contemplated the day ahead. It was Sunday, so he would send Amelia to church with Eberta, and they could pick up Mercy and George on the way. He frowned, biting the inside of his cheek, wondering what Mercy would think of him missing the service.

Why did it matter so much what she thought of him? Troubled, he tossed off the warm covers and braced for the blast of icy winter air. Teeth chattering, he pulled on his robe and slippers before charging downstairs, rubbing his hands together to keep them from going numb.

Let Mercy think what she wanted about him, Cole decided as he knelt before the fireplace in the front room. His cold fingers fumbled with the iron shovel. He uncovered last night's embers, wondering why he was letting himself care at all. He was feeling far too many emotions for his own comfort. Best to wall off his heart. Mercy was a kind lady. Amelia was lucky to have her. But that didn't extend to him. She would be basically a housekeeper with access to his charge accounts, nothing more.

So why did that image return, the silent plea in her eyes, the wordless expression of appreciation? As he slowly fed dry kindling to the glowing coals, he went over in his mind the things she'd left out of her letters, the things he'd noticed. Her well-cared-for clothing that had seen much better days. The fraying sleeve hem of her coat, the wash-worn dress, the polish on her shoes hiding a patch. George's clothes were modest, but in a newer state. Clearly she spent her money on the boy, not on herself. He wondered just how hard she'd struggled as a widow working long hours to support her son.

Wait. That wasn't his business, either. He shook his head, disappointed in his willpower. Hadn't he just told himself to stop wondering about her past? Annoyed with himself, he added a small, dry piece of wood to the grate, watched the growing orange flames lick over it, popping and crackling.

"Oh, good!" Amelia's feet drummed on the steps,

her voice echoing down the stairwells. "You're up! I couldn't sleep because I was so excited. Mercy's gonna come here today. I can't wait to show her everything."

"I'm sure you can't." He glanced over his shoulder in time to see his wild-haired daughter leap to the bottom of the stairs with a thud. "You aren't usually up at the crack of dawn. If I'd known it would have gotten you out of bed, I would have found you a new mother before this."

"No, because then she wouldn't have been Mercy." Amelia skipped across the room.

"Do I really have to remind you?" He grimaced, reached for a piece of wood and popped it into the fire. "No running in the house."

"I know, I just can't contain myself." Amelia skidded to a stop, hugging herself. "I get to walk into church this morning with a ma, just like all my friends do. I'm gonna wear the new dress Eberta made for me. Pa, do you know what this means?"

"That you're finally going to start acting like a lady?" He brushed bits of bark and moss off his hands and reached for the little fireplace broom. A few sweeps and the bits flew into the fireplace. "This getting-married thing is a good idea. You'll be getting up early, acting ladylike. It's like a dream come true."

"Honestly, Pa." Amelia rolled her eyes. "You're supposed to love me the way I am."

"Oh, sorry." He put the broom away, hiding his grin. "I didn't know. Maybe that's one of those rules we can break and toss out the window."

"Very funny." She rushed up to him, wrapped her arms around his chest and squeezed tight, tipping her head back to sparkle up at him. "Hurry up with breakfast 'cause I'm gonna be lightning fast. I get to go see Mercy!"

"I'm gonna need some mercy if you keep this up." He winced at his own pun. *Well,* he thought, *a man has to amuse himself where he can.*

"Oh, Pa." Amelia gave him an eye roll and was off, pounding back upstairs, leaving him alone in the room.

Well, looked like they'd have a few more mornings like this alone together before the wedding changed things. Only three more days until Christmas Eve, until Amelia's hoped-for ceremony. He hung up the broom, crossed the room and felt thankful to Mercy for understanding. He wasn't sure how he felt about a church wedding. He still hadn't recovered from the last one. Gritting his molars together, determined not to think of it, he veered into the kitchen, knelt in front of the cookstove and stirred the coals. When he should have been planning his morning of chores and repairs, his mind took an entirely different path.

He remembered that glint of humor when she'd been seated on his sofa, gazing up at him with part challenge, part amusement, all concealed strength.

You may tell me what to do only two times a day, she'd said with a slender arch of her brow, pure challenge and likability.

He sighed, reaching for the kindling. It was going to be hard to keep from liking her, but he was tenacious and determined. He would give it his best shot.

"Ma," George called from one of the front room windows. "Are you sure they're gonna come for us? I don't see 'em yet."

"Amelia promised they would be by." Frowning at her reflection in the bureau's small mirror, Mercy untied her hat ribbons and tried again. "I don't think they would leave us to find our own way in a strange town."

"I could help," George answered confidently. "I can see the church steeple from here. I could take you right to it, and if I got lost in the street I'd just look up to find it."

"That's a very good plan." She adjusted the bow, figured that was as good as it was going to get and raised her gaze to her face. She pinched her cheeks, hoping to put a little color in them. Too bad there wasn't something she could do about those circles under her eyes. She'd barely been able to sleep a wink, although the bed was comfortable. She pushed away from the bureau and grabbed the shawl she'd laid on the foot of her twin bed, circled around

George's bed and stepped into the hall. "What are you doing?"

"Lookin' at the horses." George's excitement seemed to fill the room with a vibrating, little-boy energy. "There's a black one. He's real shiny. What color do you think my horse is gonna be?"

"I don't know." Mercy reached for George's coat. "What color do you think?"

"Maybe brown?" George scrunched his face up, thinking on that for a bit. He took the garment she shook open for him and stabbed one arm into the sleeve, lost in thought. "There's a lot of brown horses, so yeah, he'll probably be brown. You see 'em all the time. Maybe most horses are brown."

"What if he's as white as the snow?" Seeing his collar was folded over onto itself, she pulled it out and smoothed it down. "What if he's spotted?"

"Then he'd be both white and brown." George gazed out the window, lost in his favorite game. "Unless his spots are black."

"Or red," she added, unhooking her coat from its peg on the wall.

"Or palomino, or roan or gray," George continued. "Oh, I just can't wait for my horse."

"I know, kid. It won't be much longer now." She slipped into her coat, unable to resist glancing down at the street below.

Great snowdrifts ran down one side of the street like a miniature mountain range, and because it was

Sunday no one was out shoveling the boardwalks. A few vehicles rolled by, pulled by horses struggling through the new accumulation as far from the miniature mountains as they could get. As she watched a bay team pull a sleigh past the storefront below, she realized she didn't even know what kind of horse or vehicle Cole drove. In their correspondence she hadn't thought to ask if he would provide her with a horse and vehicle. Hmm. More things to discuss later, she thought.

"Ma! Look!" George nearly shrieked, both hands splayed across the glass. "That's the best horse I've ever seen. Look. He's as white as the snow."

"And he's stopping in front of the store." She leaned in, too, feeling the cool glass against her cheek. Why her heart kicked up a crazy rhythm, she couldn't say. Something within her strained, as if longing for the first glimpse of Cole climbing down from the sleigh.

He wasn't there. A red-capped Amelia rocked her head back to gaze up at them, grinned when she saw them and waved with a mittened hand. Mercy waved back, fighting disappointment as Eberta set down the reins and hopped from the sleigh.

"C'mon, George," she said gently, strangely bereft. "We don't want to keep the horse standing in that cold."

"No, it's not good for him," he said, heading toward the door at a run.

All the way down the stairs and through the silent, echoing store, she tried to remember what Cole had written about his church life. Had he ever said he attended Sunday service? Funny, she realized as she caught sight of Eberta through the glass panes of the shop's door, busily unlocking it. She couldn't recall if he'd mentioned actually being a churchgoer himself. In his second letter to her, he'd mentioned how Amelia had commented on being the only girl in church without a mother, and Mercy had simply assumed he attended Sunday services.

Now, she could see she'd been wrong. The door opened, an icy blast of raw, wintry air whooshed in, and George bolted onto the boardwalk, eyes focused on the horse.

"Hi, Miss Eberta," he said on his way by. "Is that your horse, or is it my new pa's?"

"It's Cole's," she answered fondly, as if completely understanding the boy's love of horses. "Good morning, Mercy. I trust you slept well."

"I was very comfortable." That was the truth. She'd never slept in such a fine bed. "Thank you. I know it was you who went to the trouble."

"Oh, pshaw, it wasn't much." Pleased, Eberta relocked the door with a jangling of her keys. "Amelia wanted it nice and it's hard to say no to that girl. If you're going to be her ma, it's a skill you'll have to learn."

"I do have some practice saying no to my son,"

she answered breezily, sharing a smile with the older lady. They headed down the steps together, sinking into snow midway up their calves.

"I can see it would be hard to say no to that one, too." Eberta nodded in approval. "Someone has to take a firm hand with that girl. Not to scare you off before the wedding."

"That would be impossible," Mercy confessed, coming to a standstill in the deep snow, mesmerized by the sight of George gazing raptly at the majestic white horse, too afraid to approach the animal.

"He's the prettiest one I've ever seen," he breathed, wide-eyed and awestruck. "Is he really gonna be our horse to drive?"

"When you're with your pa," Eberta answered. "It's his driving horse. He bought you a fine mare, gentle as can be, Mercy. So you can get around and take the children where they need to be going."

"My, he *bought* a horse?" Mercy swallowed. She couldn't say why that gesture touched her. The comfortably furnished rooms, and the knowledge they would be just as comfortable in his home, were enough. "He didn't need to go to that trouble. Horses are expensive."

"You're marrying a man who can afford it." Eberta climbed onto the front seat of the sleigh. "Heaven knows that man saves every penny he can get his hands on. He's been needing a wife to spend his money for him for years."

"Oh, I didn't come to spend his money." In fact, she clearly remembered last night and his rule about the budget. "I'm used to being careful. My job didn't pay terribly, but it didn't pay well."

"And all that's behind you. Get in. George, are you going to stare at the horse or come to church with us?"

Mercy's attention was stolen by the shivering girl, trying to keep her teeth from chattering as she held out one end of the thick flannel-lined buffalo robe. Huddling under it, Amelia shook harder when cold air slipped beneath it.

Not wanting the girl to get any more frozen, Mercy slipped in beside her. "George, come sit beside me."

"I can't believe that's gonna be our horse, too." George clamored out of the snow, nearly stumbling because he couldn't take his eyes off the gelding. He dropped beside her with a fulfilled, happy sigh. "No one's ever had a horse as nice as that one."

"You'll have to ask Cole if you can pet him. And what his name is." She shook the robe over her son, tucking him in snugly. Her teeth began chattering, too.

"It's Frosty," Amelia volunteered as the sleigh jerked to a start and Frosty was off, bounding on his long legs through the sheltered part of the street, as gleaming white as the snow.

"Wow," George breathed as the animal gained

momentum. "We're in a real sleigh, Ma. Being pulled by a real horse."

"Haven't you been in a sleigh before?" Amelia asked curiously, a few strands of reddish-blond hair escaping her knit cap to curl around her adorable face.

"We owned work horses for the farm long ago," Mercy said quietly, her chest tightening at the memory. Some of the daylight seemed to drain from the sky, and she lifted her chin, determined not to let the disappointments of the past shadow this new future. "We put runners on the wagon box in the winter. That was before my husband passed on, when George was too little to remember. Those were our last horses."

"Oh, I'm sorry." Amelia seemed flustered, as if that hadn't been the answer she'd been expecting.

Leave the past where it belongs, she reminded herself. "So that's why this is so exciting for us. To be whisked to church instead of walking through the snow. And we've never been in finer company."

"I can't wait for everyone to see you." Amelia bumped Mercy's elbow gently, a show of connection. "Look, we're already turning down Second."

"I can see the steeple!" George called out.

"Will your father be meeting us?" Mercy asked quietly as they drove along, straining to search through the crowd of tethered horses and vehicles along the street in front of the church. It looked as if men gathered there, talking amiably. Although she already knew Cole wasn't one of them.

"Pa doesn't go to church anymore." Amelia shrugged, falling silent, as if there was more to the story.

Sensing sadness there, suspecting it was because of the loss of Amelia's mother, Mercy gave her a silent nod of understanding. Sometimes a broken heart simply had to find his own way.

"Look at that palomino!" George shouted, his voice high-noted with glee. "It's the most golden horse I've ever seen. Maybe that's the horse I like the most."

"I can see why." Mercy straightened George's cap, which had gone somehow askew, to keep his ears warm. It seemed every handsome horse her boy saw became his new favorite. "Eberta, I'm so glad you've come with us."

"No worries. One thing I don't miss is Sunday service." Eberta pulled Frosty to a stop at a vacant spot at the block-long hitching post. "Are all those curious eyes getting to you?"

"Why, are people looking at me?" She pulled her attention away from the men and horses, where Cole Matheson was not, and realized it was true. A circle of ladies, standing off to the side of the walkway, studied her.

Shyness washed over her and she stared at the edge of the buffalo robe feeling terribly alone. She'd been prepared to meet so many new and unfamiliar people, but she hadn't realized how at ease she'd expected to feel with Cole at her side. Not that she needed a man to lean on, goodness no, but the companionship would have felt nice. Somehow she felt terribly alone.

This was the way a marriage of convenience was, she reminded herself. And, more importantly, it was no different from how her first marriage had turned out, in the end. She pushed back the buffalo robe, folding it up for later use.

"Hi!" Amelia called out to the crowd, standing up to wave. "This is my new mother, Mrs. Mercy Jacobs, but by Christmas she will be Mrs. Matheson. And this is George."

"Hello." A friendly woman stepped forward, her blond hair tumbling out from beneath her stylish bonnet. Her smile looked familiar. "We met in the dry-goods store briefly. I'm Molly."

"Yes, so good to see you again." Like a sign from heaven, the sun chose that moment to peer between the thick mantle of clouds, smiling down on the wintry world. Mercy felt the brightness and warmth brush her cheek like an angel's touch, and it was the assurance she needed. Everything was going to be all right. "Are you here with your family?"

"See those twin girls over there?" Molly smiled at Amelia, who was hopping down from the sleigh, and nodded toward the corner of the yard, where a bunch of little girls were lying back down in the snow, making snow angels. Two identical girls with black braids hopped to their feet to admire their work. One wore green, the other blue. Molly sighed happily. "Those two are mine. Nothing but trouble, and I'd say they're about your little boy's age."

"They'll be in school together, then." She watched over George while he climbed from the sleigh and into the deep snow. He wasn't interested in the girls. He had eyes only for the horses. "Are you happy with the teacher here?"

"Why, yes, we've been most blessed with Miss Young. She's a fine teacher," Molly said, enthused. "I'm sure you'll love her. My girls do."

"That's a relief to know." Yet another one of her many worries alleviated. Mercy's smile felt wider, her spirit lighter. She glanced down at her son, who was standing half behind her, and then at Amelia, who reached out to proudly grab her hand. Such a tight grip, such a big need. Mercy prayed she could be everything the girl hoped for in a mother. What if she failed? Her chest ached at the thought; she was already in love with the girl.

"Hello, Eberta." Another woman came over, waving to the older woman.

"Howdy there, Felicity." Eberta gave the knotted rein a testing yank and, satisfied, trudged away from the hitching post. "How is that family of yours?"

"Wonderful. Tate's business is growing by leaps

and bounds, and Gertie is keeping me busy." The cheerful, beautiful woman patted her midsection gently, her condition hid delicately by the drape of her fine wool coat. "Four more months to go until this one arrives."

"You'll be even busier then," Mercy found herself adding, pleased when Felicity shared a smile with her. "Congratulations."

"Thank you. We are so happy." Felicity glowed with the truth of that statement. Mercy had never seen the like of the genuine joy and love that radiated from her when she glanced toward a dark-haired, impressive-looking man standing with the others, leaning on a cane.

True love. Mercy could feel the power of it like the sun warming the world. Once, she'd hoped for such a thing with Timothy, God rest him. Heaven knew how hard they'd tried. A touch of sadness crept in and she pushed it away. At least with Cole she would have no such disappointments, even if she would not have true love.

Who needed true love, anyway? She took George by the hand, thankful for him and Amelia—for her children. While the women chatted, leading the way down the shoveled pathway toward the open door of the church, the sunshine seemed to follow them, laying a golden path at their feet. Sign enough, she told herself, even if she felt a little lonely for more.

"That's my best friend and her ma!" Amelia

pointed out, gesturing toward a horse and sleigh pulling to a stop in front of the church. "Oh, I'm so glad you've come, Mercy. We're going to invite all of them to our wedding. And I'm glad you came, too, George."

"Uh, me, too," the boy said, glancing over his shoulder one last time at the men and horses. Mercy realized why, now that she took a more careful look. It wasn't just the horses that had captured his attention, but the men with their sons at their sides. Fathers.

Knowing she wasn't the only one wishing Cole was here, she gently squeezed George's hand.

Chapter Five

"That's our house." Amelia jabbed her arm to the north, where the prairie rose into a graceful roll of snow glittering in the sunshine.

Mercy caught her breath, staring at the proud two-story home with dormer windows on the top and a wraparound porch, light gray siding and sparkling windows surrounded by a sea of white. This was their house? She stared, not quite able to believe. Cole had described his home as modest. But it was nothing like the modest cabins and shanties they'd passed on the half-mile ride from town. It was like a dream, like nothing she'd ever thought she'd live in.

"Where's the shanty?" George asked, confused. His face scrunched up, his forehead furrowed. "Is it around back? Is that where we're gonna live?"

"No, George," Amelia said warmly, as if she already thought of him as her own little brother.

"There's no shanty. You are going to live in the house with me and Pa. That's why we're having a wedding. So we can all be a family."

A family. Amelia's words moved her heart. Mercy swallowed against the sudden lump in her throat. Her eyes stung, and she tried to blink away the unexpected tears. The girl clearly didn't know everything Cole had written in his letters, that he'd been so adamantly clear this was a formal arrangement, not a personal union.

"That sounds mighty nice to me." Mercy cleared her throat, slipping one arm around the girl to draw her closer. She did the same with George. It felt pretty fine to be seated between the children, knowing that she already had what mattered, what she'd traveled so far to find.

Well, *almost,* she thought, remembering the churchyard scene earlier and those fathers with their sons.

"Keep in mind we moved some of the furniture into town," Eberta explained as she urged Frosty along the circular drive curving in front of the steps. "The front room is a little empty, but that'll fix itself after the wedding."

"In three days," Amelia reminded them. "Don't worry, I have everything planned out."

"Your father showed me your slate."

The sleigh squeaked to a stop in front of the house. My, it was larger than she'd first thought. More impressive. The windows and porch gave it a smiling, welcoming look. Her pulse kicked up, and she tried to let it sink in. This house—a real house, not a tiny cottage like the one she and Timothy had shared during their marriage, not a shanty like the ones she'd lived in growing up and after she'd been widowed. Not in her wildest dreams had she imagined this much.

"It's not a mansion." Eberta hopped off the front seat. "But it's cozy and well-made. Cole built it himself. Did a fine job, too."

"I've never lived in a place with so many windows," she said, dazed, as she tumbled out of the sled behind Amelia. Looking up, she counted at least three bedrooms. And that was only on this side of the house.

"Ma, is this really where we're gonna live?" George tumbled from the sleigh, head tipped back, staring intently up at the second story, taking in the windows. "It's enough for lots of families."

"Oh, it's not that big," Eberta laughed kindly, patting the boy on the shoulder. "It's a nice-size family house. Don't know what you're used to, though."

"A rented shanty on the outskirts of town." Her shoes tapped on the steps as she trailed Amelia onto the porch. "This will be perfect come summer. I can plant flowers in the border beds and think how pleasant it will be to sit right here and watch the sun set."

"That's how I like to pass a summer evening." The

front door opened and Cole stepped into the slant of sunshine, dressed in a dark wool coat, his Stetson hiding his eyes, pulling on a pair of gloves. "Sounds like we are compatible on that front."

"Yes." The sight of him made her breath catch. A lump lodged in her throat. Her stomach fluttered nervously, because she didn't know how this would turn out after he'd heard what she had to say. "Amelia, I'd be most grateful if you could take George inside and show him around the house."

"Sure. C'mon, George." Amelia tromped across the porch, tossing a grin at her father on her way by. "Pa and I couldn't decide what room you'd like, so let's go pick one out."

"You mean I get my very own room?" George asked, blue eyes glinting incredulously. "Thank you, Pa."

"You're welcome." He looked right past Mercy, as if he could read her mood. His gaze landed on the boy, and that granite set to his face softened a fraction. "You go on in. Pick out your room. And try on the riding boots I brought home for you. Make sure they fit comfortably."

"Riding boots?" George froze midstride, jaw dropping. "I looked around, but I didn't see any horses here."

"Because they are on the other side of the hill." Steady and easygoing, that voice. Just like the man. "You'll be able to see them from the windows. Go on. When you're done, we'll take Frosty down to the barn and you can meet the other horses."

"You mean, you'll let me *lead* him?"

"I'll let you drive him."

The realization sank in. George gave an excited whoop. "Oh, boy. Just oh, boy!"

"You'd better hurry," Mercy advised him, relieved to see him happy again. "You don't want to keep Frosty waiting for too long."

"No, ma'am!" George earnestly charged through the doorway, feet churning, shoes pounding on the boards. The door smacked shut behind him.

"I'll be getting home," Eberta called out, circling around the corner of the house on foot. "Good luck, Mercy. I'm praying you don't need it."

"Thanks for the ride, for the company, for just everything." Mercy turned her back to Cole, leaning over the railing. "Will I see you tomorrow?"

"Count on it, missy." Eberta winked, tossed the tasseled end of her scarf over her plump shoulder and trudged around the corner of the house. A mule bayed, just out of sight. The animal must belong to Eberta, Mercy decided, startled when Cole joined her at the railing.

His dark shadow fell across her and she shivered, although he blocked the wind with his big body. Alone with him again, she was aware of every inch of his six-foot height and of her five foot three. She was unprepared for a confrontation. In the past, discussions had often not gone well with Timothy. How this would turn out was anyone's guess.

Although her stomach clenched up tight, and her palms began to sweat, she couldn't put this off. No, best to find out what kind of man Cole truly was. She fisted her hands, braced her feet, mentally preparing herself for the ordeal. "You didn't come to church."

"No, I didn't think to mention that last night." He shrugged, keeping watch as Eberta rode out of the shadow of the house on a gray mule. "You look as if you mind."

"I would appreciate you being up front with me." She watched the mule swish his tail as he walked along, heading back toward town. The sunlight blazed across the landscape, bringing the snow to life, making it shine, making it glitter. Inside she felt dark and afraid. What if by speaking up to protect George she lost him his new father? Her stomach clenched tighter at the thought. "Why don't you attend? Amelia does."

"I used to, but I stopped going." What looked like grief carved lines into his handsome face, crinkling around his eyes, bracketing his chiseled, firm mouth into a reserved frown. "I have no objection to anyone else attending. I just lost the faith for it."

"Oh." What on earth did someone say to that? She tried to swallow past the lump in her throat, wishing she knew what to do. "In truth, for the entire year after Timothy passed, I couldn't force myself to attend a single service. Not even Christmas."

"But you went back."

"I needed to. I needed faith. Life isn't the same without it." She squinted into the sun. Eberta was a shadow against the endless white. "Maybe one day you'll go back, too."

"I tried. I couldn't." His throat worked. He turned stonier, all the gentleness fleeing from his face, all the softness, all the feeling. "I tried for years until I finally gave up. It hurt too much to try. I don't plan on going back. Hope that isn't a deal breaker for you."

"What about the wedding?"

"Guess I can't disappoint Amelia, not about this, not with you." He shrugged his brawny shoulders. He looked compelling and yet rugged at the same time. Human, but unreachable. "This one time only."

"I see." She leaned against the railing, facing him, pulse skittering. "That isn't a deal breaker for me, but perhaps what I have to say will be one for you."

"I'm listening." He went rigid. Tense cords of tendons bunched in his neck. Strained muscles jumped along his jaw line as if he expected the worst.

"I understand, but George didn't." Her voice broke, betraying a tremor of emotion she hadn't meant to express. She sighed. "Today at church, he was the only little boy without a father beside him. Again. I can't tell you what it has been like watching how painful that is for him, hurting because he is hurting. For years, he's been the boy watching all those fathers and sons, wishing. Just wishing. It's been a terrible hole in his life and in his heart. I thought that was over for him, but it wasn't today."

"Oh." Cole closed his eyes. It was as if all six feet of him winced in painful realization. His dependable, wide shoulders slumped. He stared down at the toes of his boots, still as stone. "That wasn't my intention."

"I realize that now." Hands trembling, she splayed them against the wooden rail, needing something to hold on to. Relieved that he wasn't angry with her, relieved that he was very much the earnest man she'd met through his letters, she took a deep breath of the cold air. It burned in her lungs like an icy rush. "This is, after all, about the children. If there's something I'm failing to do for Amelia, you should let me know."

"Right." He nodded, staring intently down at his boots, refusing to look at her. He looked as remote as the mountains in the distance, as icy as the land mantled in snow. But when he raised his head and his gaze met hers, life shone there. She read his promise in that look, felt the solemnity of it, could see all the way to his heart. She didn't know why a son was so important to him, why he'd chosen her and George out of all the letters he must have received, but she was appreciative beyond words.

"Guess I'll figure out a way to face church. I'll do my best to make sure it doesn't happen to George again." Determination showed in the lift on his square, chiseled chin. "If it does, I'm sure you'll remind me."

"Yes, I'll be right on that. I have a sharp eye." Now she was smiling, amazed how fast that vast distance between them seemed to vanish, how quickly he could change from remote to approachable. Somewhere inside beyond all the defenses, he had a very good heart.

"Mercy!" Amelia's faint shout penetrated the outside walls of the house and the closed door. "Come see!"

"Now it's my turn," she said gently. Without realizing it, she reached out to touch the man. Her fingers landed on his arm, the act as natural as breathing. Aware of what she'd done, her breath hitched. She raised her eyes to his. She read confusion there, but he didn't move away. She did, removing her fingers from his coat sleeve, her fingertips tingling sweetly from the contact.

She felt the lingering weight of his gaze on her back as she crossed the porch and opened the door. Something had changed between them, something that went beyond words, something she could not describe. But the sun seemed to shine more brightly, the wind held less of a bite, and when she stepped into the house and closed the door behind her, the warm, friendly feeling within her remained.

"Mercy!" Amelia dashed toward her, grinning widely, blue skirts swirling around her, braids flying. "You have to see what Pa got George."

"Come look, Ma!" George's voice echoed from deeper inside the house, out of sight. "I can't believe I'm a real cowboy!"

Oh, the delight in his voice. The sound of it made her forget everything else. Her shoes tapped a merry rhythm against the hardwood floor, barely noticing her surroundings. The big gray stone fireplace, the windows letting in light and mountain views, the two overstuffed chairs in an otherwise sparse room.

A staircase rose to her right, ascending to the second floor. The kitchen was airy and pleasant, but she hardly noticed the oak cabinets and counters, the shiny new range or the round oak table seated in front of a big window. No, those details paled in comparison to the sight of her son standing by that table with a Stetson on his head and cowboy boots on his feet.

"They even fit, too!" George grinned at her, happier than she'd ever seen him. "I can't believe it. They're my very own. Amelia said so."

"Be sure and thank Cole." She blinked happy tears from her eyes, hands clasped together, just drinking in the sight of her delighted boy. "You look like a real cowboy ready to ride."

"You surely do," Amelia agreed. "Hurry, go show Pa. He's waiting to show you your big surprise."

"My horse?" George choked out, as if too overcome to say more. He hugged himself like a boy whose every dream had come true. "Oh, boy. I gotta go. 'Bye, Ma."

"'Bye, kid." She felt choked up, too. "Go and have fun with your pa."

"I will!" His boots made a hammering sound, pow-powing through the house as he made a mad dash away.

She listened to his progress, heard the door open and Cole's rumbling baritone as he said something to the boy. The door shut with a click, cutting him off. She swiped happy tears from her eyes.

"George was really excited." Amelia wandered over to the stove. "Pa is giving him an old horse to learn to ride. Howie's big, but don't worry. He's as gentle as a lamb. I wanted to learn to ride him. I begged and begged and pleaded and pleaded. I was sure I could wear Pa down and he'd agree."

"And it didn't work?" Mercy asked, amused, imagining reserved Cole's reaction to his daughter wanting to ride astride like a boy. Think how upset he got over a sled! She gave a soft huff of laughter. What a pair she and Amelia were. "Once long ago I wanted to learn to ride horseback."

"You did?" Surprised at such news, and apparently intrigued, Amelia dropped an oven mitt. It tumbled to the floor and she stooped to pick it up. "Did you ever get to?"

"Alas, no. My parents were shocked I would suggest such a thing." Mercy laughed again, love filling her at the memory of her folks, long gone now, and of those happy times long past. *Perhaps happier times could come around again,* she thought hopefully, taking in the pretty kitchen. Goodness, it was larger than her shanty. By twice, maybe three times.

"Too bad about the riding," Amelia sympathized. She opened the stove's warmer. "Have you ever gone sledding?"

"No. It looks fun." Mercy crossed over to take a look inside the warmer, from which Amelia extracted a bowl. Residual heat radiated off the stove, and it felt good. It was going to take some time to get used to the cold Montana winters. "Is this lunch?"

"Emmylou made it yesterday. She's our housekeeper," Amelia explained, carefully setting the bowl on the counter. "At least, she will be until the wedding. Then you take over."

"Ah, so in marrying me, your father is saving some money," she quipped. She liked knowing that she wouldn't be a burden to him, two more people for him to support. That was another relief. Her gaze drifted to the window, where the stretch of shining white snow and rolling meadows was broken only by precise split-rail fencing and a gray barn, trimmed in white.

A dozen horses strained against the rails, each jockeying to be the one getting petted by George. My, wasn't that a sight. She bit her bottom lip, overcome once again, watching as Cole stayed at George's side, appearing to talk gently to him, perhaps telling him about each animal. George listened intently, his little hand petting one horse nose after another, nodding solemnly to whatever the man said.

This was everything she'd hoped. Just everything.

"The palomino in the middle, the tallest horse?" Amelia leaned on the edge of the counter, going up on tiptoe straining to see what had captured Mercy's attention. "That's Howie. That's George's horse."

"My, he's mighty big." She gulped, trying not to be alarmed. That was one large animal for such a small little boy. Cole knew what he was doing, right? She gripped the edge of the counter, trying to suppress her motherly instincts until the enormous horse lowered his head and George flung his arms as far as they would go around the creature's neck. The horse, as if he were a very fine gentleman indeed, tucked the boy beneath his head protectively, as if he intended to love and look after the child.

"Emmylou left us chicken to use for sandwiches." Amelia tapped over to the pantry and flung open the door to reveal tidy shelves stacked full of food staples. "One of my chores is taking care of the chickens. In the summer, we have a big garden. And the orchard is full of trees to climb and fruit to pick."

"It sounds wonderful." Like a dream come true. Mercy glanced around, taking in the sight of her happy son and stoic husband-to-be, of her new daughter setting out a plate of covered left-over chicken onto the counter, of this home—a real house—full of sunshine and comfort and safety. She could not believe her good fortune. After working twelve-, sometimes fourteen-hour days at the hotel, day in and day out, scraping together a living, wanting better for her son, it had happened.

"I spotted a loaf of bread in the pantry," Mercy said, after one last glance at the window. "Let's get lunch made and on the table. Do you think we can tear George and your pa away from those horses?"

"It'll be tough." Amelia grinned, opening a drawer to extract a knife. "We may have to throw dessert in. Pa has a real sweet tooth."

"Good to know." Especially since she loved to bake. Maybe she could find out Cole's favorites. He certainly deserved all the effort she could give to make his life better, for what he was doing for George. The letters Cole had written telling of his life here had been no exaggeration, nor had his promises and intentions.

I don't know how I was chosen for this, Lord, she prayed, lifting the bread from its shelf. *But thank You so much. And please look after Maeve and Violet,* she added, thinking of her dear friend who was also settling into her new life. *Help all of us to find happiness.*

For the first time in a long while, that felt possible. Maybe she and Cole weren't marrying for love, but perhaps they could have a happy life helping one another. Maybe even become friends. That notion put a smile on her face as she sidled up to the counter next to her beautiful new daughter so they could make sandwiches together.

Chapter Six

"Mercy, thank you for lunch." Cole dropped his cloth napkin on the table, pushed back his chair and resisted the pull of the woman's magnetic presence. Something about Mercy kept urging him to look, to smile, to notice things about her he oughtn't be noticing. Like the Cupid's-bow shape of her lips, as blushed as new roses. Or the refined beauty of her heart-shaped face, the wide slash of her deep blue eyes, the curl of her honey-brown lashes, the dainty slope of her nose.

No, it was smarter to keep his head down, grab his hat and coat on the way to the door and not look back.

"Take your time and eat up, George." He called over his shoulder. "Come down to the barn when you're ready."

"I'm ready!" The boy hit the floor with a two-footed clatter. "Ma, Pa said he'd teach me to ride right after lunch. That I get to sit up on Howie's back and everything. I love Howie, he's my very own horse. For keeps."

"I'm sure he loves you, too." Mercy's melodic, caring words tempted Cole to look. Why she affected him, pulled at him, like this, he didn't know. Gritting his teeth, he stabbed his arms into his coat and turned his ears off to the rest of what she had to say.

If he wanted to keep not liking the woman, it would be best not to get pulled in by her, not to care. He pushed open the door and escaped into the lean-to, where his boots waited. As he jammed his feet into them, he felt the weight of her gaze on him. Had he thanked her for lunch? He searched his mind for any memory of it. Yes, he had. Shaking his head at himself, he shoved his foot into a boot. Maybe that was a sign of how worked up over her he was. Having a woman around, making the commitment to marry wasn't easy. His life was changing, and he didn't like change.

"Pa?" George's quiet voice broke into his thoughts.

Gazing down at the boy's face crinkled up into a worried, silent question, he realized he was frowning. Cole blew out a breath, replaced the frown with what he hoped was more of a grin than a grimace and patted the bench by the door.

"Need help with those boots?" he asked his son. His son. Satisfaction filled him. This was one change he liked.

"Nah, I can do it." George plopped down on the bench with little-boy exuberance, his blond hair tousled and wrangled his way into his new boots. "I'm a cowboy now."

The back of Cole's neck tingled. He turned around inexorably, as if he were destined to do it, as if he had no will or control over his own eyes. Mercy stood at the table, gathering the dirty plates, a willowy wisp of blue calico and grace.

In that moment as she stood before the window, blessed by sunlight, burnished by gold, she was no longer the stranger he'd corresponded with, widowed when her husband fell ill with diphtheria. She was no longer just the woman who'd stepped off the train, the one he'd decided was best for Amelia.

He could inexplicably see inside her, read the scars of loss that grief and hardship had made on her heart. Feel the commitment to their children. See the loneliness and the hope for a connection shadowed in those midnight-blue depths. He froze, hands fisting, unable to stop the sensation of the world fading away, the floorboards at his feet, the walls surrounding him, the children chattering.

As if in silence, as if haloed by light, there were just the two of them. Just him. Just Mercy. The emotional distance separating them vanished. His fingers wanted to unclench and reach out for hers, to take her hands in his, to ease the pain of loneliness within his own soul.

Fortunately he came to his senses in time, jerked away, turned his back and closed the door. George stared up at him, still wrestling with his second boot. Worry arched his brows and widened his eyes, as if he was frightened he hadn't been fast enough.

"It's okay," Cole soothed, knowing he'd turned away from the boy too quickly, but it wasn't George he needed to get away from. A man had to protect himself. He'd gotten by this long without being close to a woman. He saw no reason for that to change now. "Your sock is bunched up. Pull it up straight and your foot should slide in."

"Okay." George bent his head to the task, full of little-boy sweetness and intent. Task completed, he grinned and bounded to his feet.

"Button up all the way," he reminded the boy, opening the lean-to door for him. "It's cold out there."

"I know, it's not even melting." The kid tromped down the steps and landed in the snow. "If it snows like that again, will Santa be able to come?"

"Sure. Santa's used to snow. He lives at the North Pole, remember?" Cole caught up to the boy, plowing side by side with him through the drifts. "Even if we get a bad storm on Christmas, he'll make it through."

"If I were Santa, I'd have horses instead of reindeer," George commented. Up ahead several horses poked their noses out of their stalls, curious to see what was going on. Howie's golden nose was one of them. The gelding's dark eyes lit up at the sight of the boy. Howie had a soft spot for kids, and came bounding into the snow, nickering an eager welcome.

"Look, he likes me!" George clasped his hands together, overcome.

Hard not to like this kid, Cole thought, chest aching. He laid a land on the boy's shoulder. "C'mon. I'll put you on his back."

"Oh!" George trotted ahead, grabbed hold of a fence rung and pulled himself up to stand on the bottom of it. All the better to reach Howie, who arched his head over the fence, knocked George's Stetson askew and nibbled the boy's cheek with a horsey kiss.

"I love you, too, Howie." The boy's delighted giggle filled long-broken places in Cole's soul.

Maybe that was why he could suddenly feel more sharply than ever the tangible touch of a gaze on his back, how he knew Mercy stood at the window watching him with her son. His response to her troubled him, but it didn't stop him from turning nor did it stop the acres of snowy land from shrinking until it felt as if there were no distance between them at all.

This *connection* to her wasn't what he'd signed on for. This wasn't what he wanted, he thought, jaw set, hands fisting, gaze connecting with hers. His pulse fluttered in recognition of her, and an unfamiliar peace came to his soul, healing him more. Emotion he couldn't name gathered behind his eyes, burning and stinging. He felt her silence like singing. He jerked away, palms damp, the back of his neck sweating, needing the separation from her. He didn't understand what was happening, but he feared what she silently wanted.

Hadn't he made it clear in the numerous letters they'd exchanged? Mercy knew that. She'd written as much, but while that assurance had mollified him at the time, he kept worrying about it now. A woman like Mercy could find love again. She was beautiful, kindhearted and grounded, but he wasn't looking for an emotional attachment and never would be. He'd tried that before and it had destroyed his heart. He forced his gaze to focus on George, who was busily chatting with Howie and stroking the gelding's nose.

"George, let's get you up and riding." He strode to the gate and unlatched it. Several horses rushed over, friendly brown eyes searching him for any signs of food or impending affection. He waved them back, gave Patty a shove, scrubbed Chester's nose, chuckled at Polly's antics, all the while aware of the small boy behind him, who was unsure at being surrounded by so many horses.

"Don't worry, they won't trample you." He caught the child's gaze reassuringly. Funny how he remembered being younger than George, following his father into the corral for the first time. How enormous those horses had seemed back then. "They might give you a lot of kisses. And watch out, Polly will steal your hat. Wait, give that back, girl."

George laughed, which only encouraged the bay

mare to lift the hat higher, gripped lightly between her teeth, and give it a shake in the air as if to say, *come and get it.*

Ready to oblige, Cole scooped George up by the waist and held him high enough to grab his hat.

Polly lifted her head higher, stretching her neck as far as it would go, happy eyes twinkling mischievously.

"Hey!" George protested with a soft laugh. "Is she giving me sass?"

"I think she is, buddy." Cole meant to retrieve the hat for the boy, but Howie beat him to it. The big gelding moved in to bump Polly, a protective look dark in his gentle eyes. With a sigh, the game over, Polly lowered the hat into George's outstretched hands.

"Thank you, girl," he said, earning a horsey grin from Polly and a nibbling kiss on his cheek.

"That tickles." George giggled. "I think she likes me, too."

"You are charming my horses, kid." As he remembered those long-ago times, it was as if he could feel the soul of his father brushing close, feel the echo of his childhood with his pa. "You are a natural born horseman, George."

"I am?" Pleased, the boy's grin was powerful enough to change the air, warm the winds and burrow into Cole's heart.

Howie, ready to do his horsey duty, shouldered

Polly out of the way completely. No one was going to get his boy, apparently. The gelding stood expectantly as Cole hefted the child onto the horse's back. Howie nodded with approval and crooked his neck far enough around to check on the boy, as if to make sure he was sitting snug and holding on.

"See that clump of hair at the bottom of the mane?" Cole leaned in. "That's right. Hold on tight. It won't hurt him."

"I'm really doing it." No one in the history of time had ever grinned as widely or as joyfully as George as he seized a handful of mane, vibrating with excitement, ready to ride. "I'm on my very own horse. I'm riding him."

"That's right. Now sit up straight, grip him just a little with your knees, enough that you don't fall off." Cole made sure George was sitting well enough before taking hold of Howie's halter. Howie stood tall and still, full of pride and concern. Perhaps it was good for the old horse to feel loved and needed again. Every soul longed for that.

Even his own? Cole wondered, glancing over his shoulder. Mercy was gone from the window and he felt bereft, as if missing her. Which was ridiculous, he told himself with a wince. He was never traveling down that treacherous path again. He wasn't equipped to do it. He didn't have enough heart to give. He couldn't stand the thought of disappointing her.

Howie blew out his breath, impatient to move. George looked ready to burst, waiting for the horse's first step. Cole clucked, tugging gently on the rope bridle and remembering that father-and-son moment when Pa had been the one holding the bridle, leading the horse, and he'd been the boy riding for the first time. Like his own father had done, Cole kept a hand on George's knee and kept it there, making sure the boy didn't slide or fall.

"What do you think, kid?" he asked, already knowing the answer as Howie ambled along, ears pricked, turning his head to keep an eye on the boy, too.

"This is the best thing that's ever happened to me!" George looked giddy. He was an entirely different child. Unspoken were the things Cole had read between the lines in Mercy's letters, the things she hadn't said. All the opportunities George never had with no father to provide and to be there for him, all the hardships and penny-pinching and doing without.

Well, that had changed for good, Cole thought, fonder of the boy than he'd ever imagined he could be. "Hey, you really are a natural. You haven't slipped even once."

"I must be really good at this."

"Yes, you are, George." Cole assured him, remembering how his father had done the same for him. "Let's go faster. Are you ready?"

"Uh-huh."

Cole broke into a lope, and Howie smoothly transitioned into a slow cantor. The rocking movement didn't unseat the boy, although he slipped a little. Cole kept a good hold on his knee, keeping him in place.

"Ma! Do you see me?" George squealed with glee. "Look!"

"I see," sang a sweet voice, carried by the wind. "Is that a real cowboy, or is that you, George?"

"It's me!"

Mercy's burst of laughter, soft and sweet, threatened to undo him, to reach deep inside him and slip past his defenses. She was somewhere behind him on the hill, perhaps trudging through the snow to watch her son's first ride. She couldn't know what her presence did to him, how it threatened to crack his heart, the glacier it had become. He wished he had more to give her, that he was a better man. Focusing on the horse and boy, guiding Howie away to the far side of the corral, he hoped the distance would help.

It didn't. She filled his senses. The dainty crunch of snow beneath her boots, the rustle of her petticoats in the wind. The trill of her laughter, as sweet as lark song; her praise of George's riding skills, as gentle as a hymn. She was a splash of color against the white, wintry world. Golden hair, rosebud cheeks, flashing blue eyes, matching blue skirts, brown coat, purple flower on her hat. Color and life, in a way there had been none before.

And in one gloved hand, she pulled a rope attached to the front of Amelia's sled—the sled he'd forbidden the girl to use. The sled she'd bought off the Gable boy at school one day and hidden for two weeks before, while out on a delivery, Cole had spotted her speeding down Third Street with the boys. The outrage still haunted him, flaring to life when he realized Amelia traipsed behind Mercy, instructing her on the best way to ride on a sled.

His feet stopped moving while he stared in disbelief, not comprehending what his eyes were seeing. Howie halted, keeping an eye on the boy, as Mercy lifted her hand in a wave, flashed him a smile and sat down on the sled. His jaw dropped as Amelia gave a running push, let go, and Mercy—prim-and-proper Mercy, the lady he'd expressly chosen to be a model of female propriety and decorum—gave a whooping laugh as she raced down the slope, hair and skirts flying, a colorful, laughing blur against the white.

"Wow!" Amelia bellowed when Mercy had stopped at the bottom of the slope. His daughter cupped her hand to her mouth. Surely something she'd learned from the boys. "You went a lot farther than I usually do. That's like a record."

"That really was fun!" Mercy popped off the sled, brushed snow off her skirts, as if there wasn't a thing wrong with her behavior. "I can see why you like it so much. George will like this, too, I think—"

She paused, as if aware of his glowering and

glanced his way. He must be frowning fiercely again, because her face paled. She fell silent, her eyes rounding. He didn't remember lifting George to the ground or crossing the field, only that he was ducking between the fence rungs and plowing fast and hard through snow up to his knees.

"What do you think you're doing?" he demanded, letting anger take over, letting it fill him. It was better than the other things threatening to take him over. Tension coiled through him, snapping his jaw muscles tight, so tight it was hard to speak. "I told Amelia she was never to touch that sled again."

"Oh, I didn't know." Mercy took a step back, studying him as if debating whether, in his anger, he was capable of hurting her or not. Then her chin went up, as if she was a lot stronger than she looked. "You mentioned not liking that she rode her sled in town, where everyone could see. I didn't think way out here that it would matter. It's just the four of us."

"It matters," he ground out, his outrage losing steam because there was no way she could know the true reason behind his anger. And because he had that rule about keeping the past where it belonged, he hadn't told her. He was afraid of failing his daughter, of not raising her in the proper way. Angry with himself now, he realized he was towering over the woman and took a step back. "This isn't good for her, Mercy. Surely, as a mother, you know that."

"See, if you wanted to make me mad at you, you

have succeeded." Her chin ticked up a notch higher, her dark blue eyes snapping fire. "I fail to see the harm. Sledding is actually quite fun. I intend to do it again, after Amelia takes her turn."

"She's not taking a turn. She's not riding that sled."

"Fresh air and exercise is good for a girl," Mercy told him. "It's not fair that you and George get to be out here riding the horses and we can't. Hmm, maybe what we need is a sidesaddle."

"I see what's going on." He glanced up the hill, where Amelia was shading her eyes with her hands, intent on watching what was going on down below. "You two are ganging up against me."

"Not at all." Mercy's hand lit on his upper arm, a familiar, bridging touch, one meant to calm him down. It did. Her touch radiated something that soothed, a special, unnameable something that made him lean in, that made his entire being wish for what he could not have.

He stood there, mouth open, mind blank, not at all sure how to summon up one single word in protest because his brain had simply stopped working. Gaping like a fish out of water—like a man moved by a woman's caring touch—he watched Mercy turn on her heel, dragging the sled up the slope after her.

Tiny, airy flakes of snow chose that moment to come tumbling down, brushing his cheek, clinging to the sleeve where she'd touched him. The sensation of connection, of her caring concern for him, lingered.

It did not fade.

Chapter Seven

"Here are some things for George." Cole's voice echoed in the stairwell outside her rooms above the store. He hesitated in the night shadows, as if a part of them, head down, staring at the floor. Looking as if stepping into the light was the last thing he wanted to do.

"Things?" she asked quietly, curious, closing behind her the door to the bedroom where George slept. "What have you done for him now?"

"Picked out some clothes from the shelves downstairs." With a shrug, Cole shouldered into the room awkwardly and held out several folded pieces of clothing. "I noticed his things were starting to wear out. Guessing they were hand-me-downs."

"Yes." From the church donation barrel back home. Those pesky tears returned, burning her eyes and blurring her vision. She blinked them away, stepping toward him, close enough to see the dark stubble on his jaw from a day's growth. Her fingers itched to touch him there, to feel the rasp against her fingertips. It was foolish to want to get closer to him, this man who'd been clear he wanted none of that. So she squared her shoulders, tamped down the wish and took the stack of clothes he offered her.

"Brand-new." She stroked the flannel shirt, blue to match George's eyes. There were a week's worth of shirts, she noticed, and denim trousers to match. Her chest ached at Cole's thoughtfulness. "George will be thrilled. Thank you for this, for providing for him."

"Just keeping my bargain." Cole dipped his chin in an awkward bob, as if there were far more feelings behind those words than he chose to admit. "Boys his age grow like weeds. He may need underthings and socks. You can choose from the shelves downstairs, whatever he needs. Just let me or Eberta know what you take for inventory purposes."

"I will." It was very generous of him to think of so many new things for George. "This is nice of you considering I have the feeling you are upset with me. Over the sled."

"Yes, I had hoped you would side with me on the sled issue." He ambled past her and squatted in front of the cold, dark potbellied stove. The door opened with a squeak. "Guess I misjudged the kind of woman you are."

"Oh." His words hit her particularly hard. He'd

been pleasant but reserved through the afternoon and over a warmed-up supper of stew Emmylou had made the night before. But, she realized, the children had been around them. Now it was only the two of them. "I'm sorry you're disappointed in me, but I can't go against what I believe is right."

"Oh, that girls need fresh air and exercise, too?" He arched a dark brow at her, reaching for the fireplace shovel. "A nice walk wouldn't have been better?"

"It certainly wouldn't have been as much fun." She bit the inside of her lip, trying to figure out just how mad he was. Remembering how angry he'd been when he'd marched over to her in the pasture, she realized now that his upset hadn't blown over. He hadn't let it go. What she needed to do was reassure him. "You don't need to bother with the stove. It's just me, and I don't need a fire."

"So this is how you made ends meet, did you?" He ignored what she had to say and stirred the embers until they glowed bright red. He added a handful of kindling from the nearby wood box. "Once your son was warm in bed, you'd let the fire go out and sit in the freezing cold?"

"Until bedtime. To save on the cost of fuel," she said, her cheeks heating. "It was financially prudent."

"In my house, that's not the way it works." He sounded angry again, his granite shoulders tensing as he watched the tiny flames flicker and dance.

"You'll keep the fire burning until your bedtime. You'll do what I ask this time, or I'll put an end to the sledding."

As if curious about her reaction, he cut his gaze to her, studying her briefly out of the corner of his eye. Their gazes met and she felt her heartbeat pause, as if it were about to cease all together.

"You strike a hard deal, Cole," she told him, understanding dawning. He wasn't without a heart, not at all. "I'll agree to your terms."

"Good." He added small pieces of wood and, satisfied, closed the door. "At this point I wouldn't want to send you back to North Carolina. I'm rather fond of George."

He looked away, pushed off the floor and rose to his impressive six-foot height. The silence as he brushed moss and bark off his hands said more than his words ever could. His affection for George had won her devotion. He'd spent the entire afternoon teaching the boy how to ride, saddle and rein, and after supper the pair had disappeared into the barn to clean stalls and care for the horses.

"I'm rather fond of Amelia," she confessed and went quiet, too, letting her silence say much, much more.

"I'm glad." He cleared his throat and finally spoke, though he looked unsure of himself. It was endearing that for all his strength and size, he was basically shy. Why that stole her heart just a bit, she couldn't say, either.

He reached for the broom, but she beat him to it. He raised one eyebrow and his face turned to stone. She was starting to recognize his angry look.

"This is the least I can do for the man who built the fire for me." She seized the broom and swept the small amount of debris into a tidy pile. "You're going to have to get used to me doing things for you, too. I understand that it's going to be a challenge for you, as I've been alone for so long, as well."

"I see." His gaze raked over her face, and she shivered. Perhaps from the cold air, for the fire in the stove was not strong enough to begin heating the place. He sounded amused as he grabbed the nearby dustpan and knelt to hold it in place for her. "You would have been happy never marrying again?"

"It probably seems that way." She swept, sending the tiny pieces of moss and bark into the dustpan. "I would have preferred to marry, but finding someone who would be good to George was a problem."

"You had offers?" He rose, emptied the pan in the wood box.

"Several. We lived in a very small town, but every widower who came along asked for my hand." For once she was with someone who could understand her choices, unlike her friends and coworkers who'd been critical of her decisions. "One was a man who had a farm to work and five daughters. He said he'd take me on as a wife because of George, who could learn to do the work of a man in the fields."

"That's terrible." Cole took the broom from her and put it away, sympathy knelling low in his voice. "But I know men like that. They use their children as free labor."

"Yes, and that's not what I wanted for George. Better that I work long hours and have my great-aunt watch him than to expose him to that heartache." She felt surprised when Cole reached for her elbow, guiding her to the sofa, gesturing for her to sit. It had been a long time since a man had shown genuine caring for her. She settled on the cushion, telling him what she'd never told anyone. "That wasn't the worst offer I received. A salesman, who came through town regularly and stayed at the hotel where I worked, offered to make me his wife if I left George behind. Apparently he wasn't interested in raising another man's son. Nothing but trouble, he said."

"With offers like that, no wonder you were cautious with me. I was cautious, too." He shook the teakettle on the stove, listened for the sound of water in it and carried it to the kitchen nook. "It took you and me writing over a dozen letters each to reach this point. I've learned from several of my customers most folks in a mail-order situation just write a few times."

"That's what I've heard, too, but we have children. We had to be sure." She watched in amazement as

Cole filled the kettle from the water pitcher. Timothy had never done such a thing, nor had any man she'd heard of. But there he was, standing in the shadows, doing something for her. "How about you? I told you my stories. It's only fair you do the same."

"Oh, I asked a few stern-looking widows before resorting to writing an advertisement," he confessed, carrying the kettle to the stove. He set it down with a clunk. "They were all horrified. Of me, or wild Amelia, I've never been sure."

"It was you," she assured him, laughing for no reason at all. "Amelia is a gem."

"Right." Humor lit his face, softening the chiseled planes of his cheekbones and the carved line of his mouth. It drove away the shadows from his eyes, leaving a sincere openness in those depths of blue. For an instant he looked approachable, unguarded. He settled on the sofa beside her. "Yes, it must have been me. I'm told I'm a difficult man."

"No. Not difficult." She wanted to lay her hand on his sleeve, to bridge the distance between them, but it wasn't necessary. He'd never felt so close, so real. She rather liked this man. A whole lot. "Life has dealt you a blow, that's all. Sometimes we're never the same afterward."

"No, we're not." The muscles in his jaw worked. He leaned forward, away from her, planting his elbows on his knees, hands to his face. He took a moment, breathed in and out. "You must have loved your husband very much."

"I did. I married him when I was seventeen, starry-eyed and full of dreams." She hardly recognized that girl she'd been, standing at the front of the church with her friends and family watching, vowing to honor the dashing farmer who'd stolen her heart. "I was more in love with him than he was with me, I'm afraid. It took me a while to learn to see the real man, instead of the one I'd wanted to see."

"Oh, I'm sorry." He pulled his hands away from his face and straightened, his empathetic gaze searching hers. "I just assumed you had a happy marriage."

"I did, for the most part, but Timothy had his struggles." She stared at her hands, too, hesitating. "I loved him. I was devastated when he died."

"I know how that feels." He paused, letting the silence take over. But since it was broken by the rumbling of the teakettle, he got on his feet and rescued it from the stove top before it whistled and woke the boy. "When Alice passed, it was like the sun going out, never to shine again. I've been in the dark ever since."

"That's the first time you've talked about her."

"I try not to." Other than mentioning he was a widower, he'd purposefully avoided anything to do with Alice in his letters. It hurt too much. He grabbed the kettle's handle with the hem of his shirt and carried it to the kitchen nook. The darkness in the room's corner made it easier to open up. "She was my world. After the way I grew up—my father passed away from a field accident when I was about George's age. Because of our financial situation, we were about to lose the farm, Ma had to remarry. She had nothing if she didn't and three children to provide for. Her biggest fear was being homeless and us starving with no place to go. So she married a man from our church."

"That had to be so hard for her, to marry without l-love." Her words caught, as if she felt not only sympathy for his mother, but sadness for herself.

That's when he knew for sure. He could feel it in his gut. Deep down, Mercy was hoping for a connection between them, for something more than a simple, courteous convenient marriage. Troubled, he measured tea into the ball, hands shaking. Tea leaves likely fell onto the small table, but it was too dark to see them. He dropped it into the teapot and reached for the kettle.

"It was a hard sacrifice Ma made." He listened to the water pour, rushing into the pot. Telling by ear when it was full. He set the tea kettle aside, aching in a way he couldn't describe. He hung his head, drew in a breath and hoped—no, prayed—he was wrong about Mercy's hopes.

"The man Ma married was well-thought-of by many, but we saw his true colors." He did his best to keep at bay those old memories of the scared and vulnerable boy he'd been, struggling to hide his wounds from his ma. "My stepfather was brutal. I was the oldest, so I made sure I bore the brunt of it."

"To protect your younger siblings," she said, as if she'd memorized every fact he'd ever written during their correspondence. Not only committed them to memory, but to her heart. Her caring warmed the air, drove back the shadows, made her lovelier than ever. "Is that why you are so good to George?"

"Partly." He reached down a mug from the shelf and held himself very still. The truth—the admission—didn't come easily. "Alice died in childbirth. Our son was stillborn. She lived long enough to see his face and then she was gone, too."

"Oh." Shocked silence followed. Mercy bowed her head, as if she'd been struck. "I'm so sorry. I had no idea. That had to be unbearable for you."

"Unbearable," he repeated. It was the closest word to what he'd gone through. He'd nearly died of sorrow, too, but Amelia had been three years old and he'd had to find a way to go on. "My heart broke for the final time that day. I walled off the pieces, picked myself up and I'm still getting by the best I can."

"And so that's why you want a convenient marriage." Her soothing, sympathetic tone reached out to him. She studied him over the back of the sofa, her beautiful face soft with understanding.

He'd never seen anything more lovely or compelling. He didn't know why he could see inside to her heart or why he could read it so easily. But he saw there the dashed hopes for an emotional connection between them, the sorrow for his lost wife and son, and the understanding of what his heart had been through. Without a word, he nodded, acknowledging what he'd seen in her. She smiled sadly, knowing what he meant.

"That's why I was so interested in you," he confessed, reaching for the teapot and filling the cup. "You'd lost a husband, so you know what it's like. And you had George."

"Yes, George." Her tone came falsely bright, layered with too many emotions to name. "You are a blessing to him."

"As he is to me." He carried the cup toward the light, toward her, and gave it to her. "I can't tell you what this afternoon meant. Teaching him to ride. Watching him discover the joy of having a horse. I hope what I gave to him had at least as much value as what he gave to me today."

"More." She blew on the tea to cool it, because she needed time to gain control of her emotions or she wouldn't be able to hide the most private ones from him. "George was floating he was so happy. I've never seen him like that."

"Good." As if buoyed by that, Cole nodded, sank onto the edge of the sofa and steepled his hands. Half in the shadows, half in the reach of the lamp's light, he made a stunning image of light and dark, of strength and heart. "I think George and I are going to get along just fine."

"I do, too." She took a sip of tea, although her hand was trembling so it wasn't easy. She burned her lip, scorched her tongue, and spilled some on her dress. None of that mattered next to the enormous swell of affection and grief filling her. "If you could have seen him before, watching our neighbors back in North Carolina. Mr. Fulton would be out in the alley playing catch with his sons or in the backyard rubbing down their horse, and the yearning on George's face would make me cry every time. You've done something for my boy, something you don't even know."

"I do." His throat worked, the tendons cording with the strain of his emotions. "I've been yearning for a son, too."

Tears filled her eyes, thinking of the hole in Cole's life, the son he never got to know. She blinked hard, willing those tears back. Too bad she couldn't do the same with her affection. It welled up, unbidden, rising through her like hope on the darkest winter night, like starlight in a cold Christmas sky. She took another sip of tea, swallowing the hot liquid blindly, ignoring the scald. How could she not love the man who loved her son?

"Well, I'd better go." Cole stood, lost in the shadows again. He moved in the darkness, a shadowed line of his shoulder, a curve of his capable hand. "Like I said, be sure and take what you need from the store, for you, the boy or the house. I expect you to make the place your home, any way you want. Amelia made an appointment for you at Cora's dress shop tomorrow."

"Oh, for the wedding dress." She thought of the slate, of the girl's hopes written out in a tidy, organized list. Quite extravagant, but now she understood. As George had longed for a father, as Cole had longed for a son, so Amelia had yearned for a mother and a wedding to celebrate it. "Of course. Anything Amelia wants."

"Within reason." Cole's firm tone held warmth, too. "No sledding in town. No horse riding. No Stetson. She keeps threatening to trade in her sunbonnet for one."

"I'll do my best." Mercy set the cup aside and rose, too, trailing after him to the door. The affection she felt for him seemed to keep expanding, growing beyond all bounds. She prayed she could keep it secret from him, to be the wife he wanted and deserved. "I'm worried about what Amelia wants for my wedding dress versus what you can afford."

"I've already spoken to Cora about that." The door whispered open and he stood in the darkness before it, towering over her, close.

So close.

Her skin tingled sweetly, as if a mellow summer breeze had blown over her. She lifted her chin and swallowed, praying her feelings didn't show in her voice. "Good. I've never been dress shopping in a store before. Growing up, Ma always made our clothes and so I've always made mine."

"How old is that dress you're wearing?" he asked, his tone firm and caring at the same time.

"I sewed it when Timothy was alive." The last time she'd been able to afford fabric for a new dress.

"That's been a long while," he commented. "At least four years."

"Five, but it's quite serviceable. It still has another good year left. Maybe more."

"Sorry, that's not going to happen." He gave a soft bark of surprised laughter. He couldn't believe this woman. She thought of the children before herself. She really didn't realize that he'd wanted to better her life, too, not only Amelia's and George's, when he'd written his proposal. Something about her had hooked him. Now he knew what. "I told Cora you need more than a wedding dress. You need a new wardrobe."

"Oh, no. Absolutely not." She sounded scandalized, horrified. "That would be a terrible expense."

"It's mine to pay," he reminded her. "Remember my second rule?"

"Oh, yes, the budget. How is this living on a budget? It's too extravagant." She truly sounded distressed. The reaches of the lamplight strained to find her, to highlight the golden glints in her hair, to caress the curve of her face. Crinkles dug into her forehead as she gazed up at him. "No, that makes no sense. I told you in our correspondence. I don't need anything. I'm not the one in need."

He begged to differ. He looked at her and saw all kinds of need. The need for her son, for a home, for family and for love. That was the one that stabbed at him, that cut like a blade. It was the one thing he could not give her. The one thing he did not have to give.

It saddened him greatly, because he wanted so much for her, for this woman who'd given him a son and who'd made his daughter happy. He still could hold on to the hope that she'd help mold Amelia into an acceptably behaved daughter. After all, a man had to hold on to something.

"It doesn't matter," he told her, his chest hurting so stridently it was as if he'd been kicked in the ribs by seven wild horses. "I'm the head of the household. I'm the man. What I say goes. You'll get new dresses. End of story."

"I thought we agreed not to boss each other around?" Amusement tugged her pretty mouth upward, and there was a hint of challenge in her eyes.

He liked this woman. Very much. "Sure, we agreed to that, but that doesn't change the fact that I'm in charge. On this matter, you need to do what I say."

"Buy myself dresses I don't need?" Her amusement faded; the challenge remained. Her delicately carved chin hiked up another notch. "I'm not in need."

"Yes, you are." She'd been struggling in poverty for too long and that was over. The overwhelming need to take care of her, too, rushed through him like a flash flood, knocking down some of the barriers he'd had up for years. Thankfully some of his defenses stayed standing, the iron-strong ones, the ones closest to his heart. "You will be a store owner's wife, and how you dress reflects on me. You need to look the part."

"You're just saying that. I don't believe you mean it." Her chin dipped, as if she, too, could look inside him and see the truth.

His fingers reached out on their own accord to curl around her delicate chin. Her skin felt warm and silken-soft as he nudged her chin up so their eyes could meet. She was a woman of pride. He saw that, and he saw, too, what his gesture meant to her. No more patched dresses, faded from years of washing. No more quiet desperation struggling to make basic ends meet. They were a team, meant to help each other.

"I mean it," he told her, pretending to be tough when he was crumbling. His ribs felt broken, his internal organs ripped and bleeding. How could feelings hurt so much? "I won't go around town overhearing folks talking about how ragged my wife's clothes are. I deserve better than that."

"So, buying new things is a wifely duty?"

"Yes. Glad you understand me." His throat closed up, overcome by the cracking pain inside him. He hated the emptiness he felt within, the void of his lost heart, the one that Alice and their son had taken with them when they'd passed. With no hope of getting it back, he felt like a failure, feared the disappointment to come. But did that stop him from leaning forward? No, not one bit. His lips brushed her forehead with the faintest touch. He breathed in her rose and soap scent, and the emptiness inside him throbbed like an open wound.

That kiss was a mistake. Reaching out to her at all was a mistake. Ashamed of himself, of what he'd done, he turned away and strode out the door. What was she expecting now? That there might be more kisses in their future, more closeness, even love? He winced, knowing he would fail her. He had nothing to give to her.

"Good night, Cole." She broke the silence, sounding practical, like the woman from the letters he'd come to trust. As if she knew his heart, her voice consoled. "I can't tell you how much I'm looking forward to spending your money tomorrow."

A joke. That helped, he thought, feeling the pain within him ease. He managed a grin as he caught hold of the doorknob, crossing over the threshold. "Now I'm actually feeling like a married man."

"Excellent practice for the real thing," she teased back.

"Wait, I'm thinking about changing my mind." He winked, but it was too dark for her to see or to realize he was telling the truth. Like a wounded man, he headed down the stairs, his gait unsteady, feeling winded and reeling from the sort of pain that comes from a wound that had never healed.

"Sorry, no changing your mind now," she gently kidded, her voice echoing down the stairwell. "Not when I finally get to spend your money."

While her words were light and breezy, meant to make him smile, there was something else there. An emotion he sensed, an awareness. He'd not hidden his true feelings from her, after all.

He grimaced, alone at the foot of the stairs, as the door closed, blocking off all sight of her. He turned around, staring up into the deep shadows, feeling the night's cold wrap around him. He longed for her the way the dark yearned for light. He wished he had a heart to give her.

Chapter Eight

"Yep, that's the dress," Amelia declared with a decisive nod in the sunniest corner of Mrs. Cora Jones's dress shop. The girl gave her braids a toss. "I knew it the second I saw it in the front window. It makes you even more beautiful, Ma."

Ma. Mercy's hand flew to her throat. She would never get over how good that felt. She smiled at her daughter, held out the green skirt and slowly twirled. "Isn't it a little festive for a wedding? I was expecting something sedate and very somber."

"Oh, no, this is just right." Amelia tilted her head to one side, considering, absolutely serious. "It's a Christmas dress. See the sprigged holly on the bodice? And the velvet skirt is my absolute favorite. Pa won't let me wear velvet. He says I'm too young, but I'm dying to."

"Perhaps together we can sew a dress for you. I'm

thinking we can find a way to put some velvet on it." Loving that idea, Mercy turned to eye the plentiful bolts of fabric in this upscale shop. She'd never stepped foot inside such a fancy establishment before or worn a dress like this, with mother-of-pearl buttons and trims of dainty lace and silk.

"Why, that looks lovely on you." The shop owner bustled over with genteel grace and genuine friendliness. "The perfect dress for your wedding in, what, two days?"

"One and a half now," Mercy said shakily. "It's counting down more quickly than I thought."

"A Christmas wedding is terribly romantic." Cora Jones selected a red velvet bonnet from the nearby display and set it on Mercy's head. "I met my husband during the Christmas season. It's a time for joy. I've known Cole a long time. You couldn't have found a more wonderful man."

"I think so, too." Mercy squinted at herself in the full-length mirror, hardly recognizing her reflection. Was she really this woman with a twinkle in her eye, looking slender and elegant in a finely tailored, fashionable dress? Her cheeks were rosy, her skin glowing. She felt so full of life.

The last time she'd felt this way had been her first wedding day. The realization slammed into her, forcing the air from her lungs. She gasped, covering her mouth to hide her dismay. No one noticed. Amelia was busy conferring with Cora about the hat.

Cora had turned around to choose a different bonnet. Mercy felt her heart break, remembering that girl she'd been, so full of hope. Love hadn't turned out quite like she'd expected. She and Timothy had struggled, and while they'd loved one another, they'd grown apart a little more each year of their marriage. She'd longed to be closer, working hard to repair the distance between them up until death took him.

Love and marriage were complicated and not easy, and she'd loved Timothy deeply. Her grief had healed over time, and a new wish had taken hold of her, that one day she would find love again, but this time with a man who loved her at least as much as she loved him. That it could be even better next time around. Of course, it had been only a hope. George's welfare and happiness came first, which was why she'd agreed to look for a husband when she'd caught the boy climbing down from the backyard tree last summer, wiping tears from his eyes. It hurt not having a pa, he'd said. Agreeing to find a good man to marry hadn't been about her dreams.

It had been about George's. Her gaze went to the front window, where the boy was visible bundled in the new winter coat Cole had let him choose from the dry-goods display. George was keeping their mare company, the one Cole had bought for her and given to her earlier in the day. George's blue knit hat bobbed around as he petted Polly's nose. The red mare, the gentle lady she was, patiently kept her head low so the boy could easily reach her.

Mercy slipped off the hat and handed it to Cora, who had consulted with Amelia to choose a dark green velvet bonnet. As Mercy took it from them and angled the simple, tasteful hat onto her head, she watched a boy approaching on the boardwalk wave to George. They looked to be about the same age. The other boy had his mother with him. They appeared to be Christmas shopping, judging by all their packages. The boy greeted George with a smile and they instantly started talking as if destined to be friends, the new boy petting Polly, too.

Yes, this was everything she'd hoped for her son. What were her needs compared to that?

"That's perfect on you," Cora breathed. "You're a vision."

"I've never seen anyone so beautiful," Amelia agreed. "Not ever."

"You're sweet." Mercy gathered the girl in her arms and gave her a quick hug. Definitely sweet. "What about you? Do you have a special dress for the wedding?"

"We already have that taken care of." Cora patted a wrapped bundle on the counter behind her. "Now that we have a dress for the wedding squared away, we need to get you some everyday things."

Mercy started to protest, but then she remembered how important this was to Cole. Last night he'd broken her heart with his story. She'd seen a side of the man that moved her still. Last night, he was all she'd thought about when she'd been tossing and turning, trying to sleep. All through the morning he stayed on her mind as she'd gone about wedding preparations and Christmas-type errands in town. She couldn't forget the brush of his kiss to her forehead, so infinitely gentle, making her fall in love with him even when she knew there was no chance he could ever return her love.

A kiss on the forehead was all the affection she would ever receive from him.

But this wasn't about her, she reminded herself. It was about George and Amelia. Another glance at the window told her George's new friend had moved on, but he appeared happier, smiling away as he petted Polly.

"Ooh, finding new dresses for you is gonna be so much fun," Amelia said, diving toward a rack of lovely winter dresses. "Hmm. George is gonna get real cold if he stands out there for much longer. Mrs. Jones, would it be all right if I got him a cup of hot chocolate?"

"Absolutely." Cora brightened as if she liked the idea very much. "In fact, I'll be happy to make you both a cup. Mercy, would you like some, too, or would you prefer a cup of tea?"

"Tea, please." She took one last took in the mirror as she removed the bonnet. The Lord had answered every one of her prayers. He'd found a good husband for her and a fine father for George. They had a safe home, plenty of food, basic necessities met. They even had Howie and Polly.

I'm so thankful, Father, she prayed silently, her gaze fastened on the window and on her son. *Am I wrong for wanting more?*

She felt that way. She felt selfish, when as a mother her only concern should be her two children. As if heaven agreed, the sunshine chose that exact moment to dim, fading away to gray shadow. The first snowflakes fell, chunks of white plummeting straight to the ground. No-nonsense, as if driven by a sense of duty.

It felt like an answer.

"So *thrilled* for you, Cole." The young Mrs. Ruby Davis beamed at him from the other side of the store's front counter. "Eberta told me all about your upcoming marriage. Best wishes to you."

"Thank you." He did his best to force a smile, as he'd done throughout the afternoon whenever a customer had gushed about his good fortune. Looked like he'd best give Eberta another talking-to or she'd be unstoppable, telling any customer who would listen about his impending marriage.

He grimaced, handing over the new bride's purchases. Happiness lighting her up, Mrs. Davis accepted the package, likely a Christmas gift for her husband, Lorenzo. She looked like the very picture of what a joyful wife should be, and it brought to the forefront all his doubts.

"Merry Christmas, Cole!" Ruby said over her shoulder on her way toward the door. "I'm looking forward to meeting your bride."

"So am I." A woman with a heart-shaped face, curly brown hair and compelling eyes stepped up to the counter and plunked down a bundle of wooden train tracks from the toy section. Mrs. Christina Gable, glowing from her pregnancy, radiated another kind of happiness he remembered well.

And reminded him of the man he'd become. He was aware of that a lot lately, he thought as he tore paper off the roll to wrap the purchase. The nearness he'd allowed with Mercy yesterday troubled him. It had been too close, too familiar, too everything. Frowning, he handed the package back to Christina Gable and reached for his account book.

"What a blessing a new wife will be for you," Mrs. Gable said kindly. "You've been alone for so long."

"Intentionally," he said without thought, wincing because the truth felt so harsh.

"Broken hearts can mend," she merely said, as if he hadn't been rude at all. She tucked her package under her arm, understanding etched into her face. "Remember that. Maybe the best is yet to come in your life."

"Merry Christmas," he said with a nod, ignoring

the wrenching crack of pain in his chest. Thinking of Mercy and a future with her made him hurt with the same strident, unrelenting pain of his long-ago grief. He gritted his jaw so tightly his teeth ached. That was a good thing. It distracted him from his troubles.

"That's the last customer of the day," Eberta announced the moment the door closed behind Mrs. Gable, and she turned the lock. "Whew, what a day we've had. My feet are complaining."

"You're welcome to quit at any time." He scribbled Mrs. Gable's purchase onto her account and closed the ledger. "It would be preferable to you telling everyone in this store about my wedding."

"Why wouldn't you want everyone to know?" Eberta asked slyly. She knew him well enough to guess why he'd been silent all day, except for necessary conversation with customers. She tapped toward him, concerned. "You're having second thoughts, aren't you?"

"No, not second thoughts." He tucked the ledger into place on the back shelf. "Fifth, sixth, seventh thoughts maybe."

"I see." Eberta sighed heavily, her disappointment in him echoing in the store. "What about Amelia? What are you going to tell her?"

"I haven't decided for sure." The pain behind his ribs wrenched harder at the thought of disappointing his daughter. Of having to let go of George. The children weren't the issue.

Mercy was.

"Well, you think long and hard before you turn away that nice woman." Eberta's tone held a note of understanding. She'd been his employee back then, too, stood beside him during the double funeral where they'd lowered his wife and his son into the ground.

Emotion clogged his throat and he swallowed hard, trying to force it down. But the sorrow stayed. He'd never had the strength to deal with it. The grief had been too huge, too much to handle; it would tear him apart, destroy him, leaving nothing of him.

So he coped by turning to his work. He opened the small closet door behind the counter and hauled out a broom and dustpan. "I'll take care of cleanup. You get home before the storm worsens."

"A little snow won't hurt me, I'm too tough for that." Eberta marched around the counter and stole the broom from him. Her jaw was set, but her gaze compassionate. "I insist on closing up and I won't take no for an answer. Amelia is waiting for you. George will be there. Mercy is fixing supper."

Oh. His step faltered. He hung his head. She'd been haunting him all day, sneaking into his thoughts, tormenting him. And that kiss. He'd let his guard down too far last night. He was in danger of letting her in. In the decade since he'd become a widower, no one—*no one*—had gotten this close.

At a loss, he blew out a breath, fisted his hands and unfisted them.

"Thanks for all your hard work today." The words croaked past the tightness in his throat as he headed toward the back door. The frantic urge to stay and keep working, to remain busy to delay the inevitable, overtook him, but Eberta was right. He needed to go home. He had to figure out what the right thing to do was—and he feared it wasn't marrying Mercy.

In the back room, he shrugged into his coat, hardly noticing what he was doing, and launched out the door into the alley. Thick, busily falling chunks of snow hailed toward the ground, and he knuckled down his hat to shield his face. Mercy. He wasn't looking forward to facing her. The sick feeling in his gut told him he already knew what he had to do.

She was young and beautiful, and regardless of what she'd agreed to, she wanted a loving marriage. She deserved that. As he trudged down the alley between buildings toward the intersecting street, snowflakes struck his face like tears. He cared about her. He couldn't help it. Last night, talking with her, sharing his painful past, had opened up a door to that pain he could no longer close. He could not live like this day after day, with the agony of what he'd lost wringing him out over and over.

"Why, it's Cole Matheson," a friendly voice called out. Reverend Hadly climbed out of his sled in front of the livery stable. "I was just thinking about you and your upcoming wedding. Christmas Eve ceremonies are my favorite. There's something special about them on such a sacred night."

"I agree." His throat closed up and he was barely able to squeeze out the words. Seeing the minister reminded him of the commitment he feared he couldn't make. That failure troubled him. "I hope you are on your way home. The temperature is dropping."

"It surely is. I'm trying to keep my teeth from chattering. Now, what about you?" Hadly's round face crinkled with concern. "You look troubled. It's natural to have a hard time moving on. Amelia brought Mercy by the church this morning, and anyone can see she is a gift from God. A much-needed blessing for your life."

"God doesn't need to bless my life." The confession felt like an anvil on his chest, the truth of it was something he'd kept inside since he'd lost wife and baby. "I'm fine. I don't need anything. It's the children who matter."

And Mercy. He ached more thinking of what he couldn't be for her. He could not be what she needed, what she deserved. He'd lost his heart, so he could not love her. He was no longer a man capable of deep feeling. He swiped snow off his lashes and spotted one of the stable workers, who nodded at him and disappeared, hurrying to fetch Frosty. Another appeared to take the reins of the reverend's horse.

"An arrangement for the children's sake can be a

blessing for you, too." Hadly brushed snow off his hat, turning to head home. "Maybe God has been waiting all this time to bring the right woman into your life. He knows your heart."

Then He knows my failings, Cole thought, watching the veil of snow close around the minister, stealing him from sight. The jingle of a harness speared his attention. The sight of his gelding clomping toward him, led by the stable worker, reminded him of where he was headed next. Home. There was no more delaying it. No more denying it.

He mounted up, riding bareback through the outskirts of town. The driving snow chilled him and hastened Frosty's quick gait along the snowy road. When he'd proposed to Mercy, he'd imagined her to be hardened by the world, weary of hardship, content to find the sanctuary of a convenient marriage and a good home. From her letters, she'd sounded like a practical, no-nonsense kind of lady. A good mother, gently spoken, proper to a fault.

Just what he'd been wanting. Instead, he'd gotten a beautiful young woman full of hopes and full of life. He could still picture her zipping down the hillside on Amelia's sled, skirts flying. The music of her laughter, the pull of her heart on his, the way she'd dismantled half of his defenses with a single, caring touch. She was tearing his world apart.

Worse, he acknowledged as the countryside rolled by, she was tearing him apart.

The house came into view on the knoll just outside of town. The windows glowed golden with lamplight, drawing him like a candle in the darkness, the only light by which to see. He rode close enough to spy a figure pass in front of the kitchen window and linger.

Mercy. *She must be preparing supper,* he reasoned, noticing the way she leaned slightly forward, intent on a task before her. Light gleamed on her blond hair, polished the lovely curve of her cheek, highlighted her soft full bottom lip as she turned to smile at someone else in the room. Likely his daughter. Mercy's face lit, radiating a mother's love. Nothing could be more beautiful. His pulse stammered, affected, and his heart vibrated with agonizing pain.

It was too much. He tore his gaze away, dismounted and led Frosty into the barn. The horses, who'd retreated to their stalls for shelter from the storm, poked their heads over their gates to welcome him with neighs and nickers and curious eyes. Howie looked especially dapper, his brown gaze shining with happiness. Cole didn't need to guess why. Clearly George had spent part of the day with him.

As he put up Frosty and closed the rest of the horses into the barn, he held himself as still as he could, letting his broken heart rest. No thinking of Mercy, or the wedding or the decision he had to make. He shook his head, bit his lip. How could he marry her like this? He could not be what she wanted, and he was sorry. Very sorry. He didn't even know how to be the man of deep feeling he'd once been, when he'd been whole, when wife and baby hadn't taken the best part of him with them. He was left with the shell of the man he used to be, and it was no good for anyone. Not Amelia, not George and especially not Mercy.

He'd wanted a wife to step in and be the parent he could not be, caring and involved, emotionally there for Amelia. At her age and with the changes of womanhood coming, she needed that. But he couldn't endure a wife who reminded him of the emptiness within him, the hollow place that remained where his heart used to be. Where his love used to be.

He couldn't endure the knowledge of what that would do to Mercy.

The minute he stepped foot outside the barn, closing the doors behind him, her light drew him through the storm. He tried not to look up; he tried not to be moved by her. The anguish inside him strengthened until it felt as if every bone he owned was breaking. Snow tapped against his hat, brushed his cheek, clung to his coat as he marched up the hill toward the house. The minister's words stayed with him, too. *She is a gift from God. A much-needed blessing for your life.*

A blessing shouldn't hurt, he thought, his mind reaching upward as if in prayer. The God he still believed in would not lead him to more pain.

He stepped into the fall of light from the front

window. Standing on the steps, ready to knock the snow from his boots, he saw into the house. A green spruce tree stood proudly in the drawing room, grandly holding up paper chains and popcorn strings on its evergreen boughs. George went up on tiptoe to hang a paper snowflake by a yarn loop. The boy bit his bottom lip, button face scrunched up in thought, before choosing the exact spot he wanted for the decoration.

Amelia breezed into view, bubbly and bouncing, happier than he'd ever seen her. Relaxed, delighted, somehow more mature and elegant as she handed George another snowflake to hang. The boy took it gladly and the two of them contemplated where to place it. At their feet lay brightly wrapped presents tied up with ribbons and adorned with bows. The scene looked like something out of a Christmas dream.

This was Mercy's doing, Cole thought, hand to his chest, grimacing at the soul-breaking crack of his heart. She was changing everything with her love and gentle kindness. Bringing life back to his house, bringing Amelia to her better self, making a home for her son.

Mercy waltzed into sight, resplendent in a new dress, obviously from Cora's shop. The finely tailored garment, as red as a holly berry, skimmed her slender shape and brought out lustrous red tones in her blond hair. She looked taller somehow, as if no longer bowed down by hardship, her beauty more radiant. Joy polished her with a rare luster.

The sight of her changed him. The faint, muffled lilt of her laughter penetrated the walls and seemed to burrow within him, touching his agonized heart. He swore he felt a hand on his shoulder, a touch of reassurance, but when he looked there was no one there, nothing but the snow.

The rending of his heart deepened. It felt as if he were breaking all the way to the bottom of his soul. He splayed a hand against the siding, holding himself up when the pain became excruciating. Tears burned behind his eyes, and he realized it was not tears, but feeling. Emotion, raw and pure and true. The last stone walls around his heart fell, tumbling and crashing into bits, leaving the broken emptiness within him exposed.

"Cole." Mercy's voice, muffled by the wall, drew him, and when he looked up she was crossing toward the door, her loving smile the most beautiful thing he'd ever seen.

Or felt.

The door whisked open, and the warmth and light of home tumbled over him like grace. Mercy smiled up at him. "You're home."

"Pa!" two children cried out, turning to run at him, pounding across the room.

But his attention remained on Mercy, her quiet welcome saying so much more. When her hand lit on his sleeve, he felt everything. The gentle weight of her touch, the impact of her caring, the potential of her love. The world was no longer filled with ice and snow, but with merriment and hope, with children running to throw their arms around him and pull him into the house, talking over one another telling him about their day and the tree and the decorations.

The sensation lifted from his shoulder, leaving him alone, his heart whole. He realized the pain had been his heart coming to life, that he was no longer empty. That the pain was gone and Mercy was there, so he took hold of her hand. Her surprised gaze met his and without words, without the need for them, he knew she felt with her heart what he could not say.

Epilogue

Christmas Eve

"Look, Ma!" Amelia breathed incredulously at the blaze of lights gleaming through the church's windows as the sleigh eased to a stop at the hitching post. "Everyone must have come for the wedding, just as I hoped. Oh, it's gonna be beautiful. Just beautiful."

"Yes, it is." Mercy glanced behind her to the two children tucked into the backseat, bundled beneath warm furs to keep out the evening's chill. "How could it be otherwise? Tonight we become a real family."

"The best Christmas present ever," Amelia declared.

George wearing his new suit, nodded enthusiastically, too overcome to speak.

Yes, this was the best Christmas present. Joy

warmed her up, chasing away the icy winds and the snow drifting down from the heavens. She smiled at the man seated beside her, who took her hand in his.

"Are you ready for this?" he asked, his tone rumbling with caring, with the kind of regard she'd never dreamed of finding. He chuckled. "We can delay a few more minutes, if you're feeling nervous."

"Not nervous. Not at all." How did she begin to describe the way she felt? The moment when he'd walked through the door yesterday, his shadows gone, his heart whole and healed and shining in his eyes, she'd felt her world shift. Her soul had come alive as if for the first time. They'd decorated the tree together as a family. They'd laughed, they'd joked, they'd been closer than ever. And still were. "I can't wait to become your wife."

"I can't wait, either." His hand engulfing hers squeezed gently, letting her know he meant every word. His gaze fastened on hers, full of promise of a future made new. She saw the years roll by, laced with their children's laughter, with love and togetherness. There would be more babies, happy memories to be made and above all, the devotion and tenderness of a man who loved her with all the depths of his heart.

Just the way she loved him.

"You kids go on inside," Cole said with a wink. "I want to say a few things to your ma before we go in.

There won't be a chance, what with all those people Amelia invited to our wedding."

"And they're all waiting for you, Pa," Amelia reminded him as she tossed off the robe. "C'mon, George. This will be mushy, anyway. We don't want to hear it. Besides, there are some boys your age in the church, I'm sure. I'll introduce you. They like to sled, too."

"Okay!" George said, bouncing into the snow with her. "I'm hopin' Santa brings me my own sled."

"I have a good feeling he will," Amelia answered, heading off in the snow at his side.

"We'll have to see about that," Cole said, rolling his eyes, although he knew Mercy had already chosen a sled from the store for George. It seemed he was going to have to learn to live with the sledding.

But as he gazed upon his remarkable wife-to-be, he didn't mind. All he could ever want was right here. He folded back the robe and helped her down from the seat. The children ran ahead, leaving them behind in the darkness and snow. It drifted down like grace, like hope, and he could feel the change in his heart, the awareness of the grace he'd been too broken to feel. It was everywhere around him, sweet and saving and renewing. He was thankful it had renewed his heart. So very thankful.

Mercy had done that, too. He turned toward her, the calm places in his soul filling. She looked beautiful tonight, as a bride should, in a fancy green hat, bundled up warmly in her new gray coat and matching scarf and mittens. She took his breath away. She was his heart.

"What did you need to say to me?" she asked as he shook out Frosty's blanket and covered him with it. Not one to be idle, she tethered the gelding to the hitching post, granting him several nose pats in the process.

"Oh, the usual thing a man says to the woman he's about to marry." He shrugged, bending to secure the buckle beneath Frosty's belly. "This is a big step we're about to take."

"Yes, I've been certain about you from your first letter. I saw how much you loved your daughter, how glad you were I had a son." She looked vulnerable with the snow tumbling all around her, airy and sweet, like little pieces of heaven. "But I never dreamed it would be as good as this."

"Me, either." Done with his task, he patted Frosty's shoulder and turned toward his bride. Emotions—hope, faith, joy—filled him, but one outshone all the others for it was the most important of all. He drew her close, brushed snowflakes out of the wisps of gold framing her dear face. That emotion rushed through him without end, without limits. "I love you, Mercy."

"I love you." She gazed up at him, affection deepening her blue eyes, unmistakable and true. "I will always love you."

"Not more than I will always love you." He offered her his arm. "Let me escort you to the church. If you're ready to marry me, that is."

"I'd run if the walkway wasn't so icy." She looped her arm in his and they took off together, marching toward the light and merriment, to friends gathered to celebrate their marriage. Their real marriage. Not one of convenience. Not one of duty.

But of love. That was the best gift of all. Bliss filled her as she climbed up the steps and into the shelter of the church's foyer, with Cole at her side. How wonderful he was, holding the door for her, helping her with her coat, hanging it up for her, gazing at her as if she was his greatest blessing.

No, *bliss* was too small of a word for what she felt, and for what waited her as his wife.

"What's that?" Cole asked, gesturing toward the sprig of mistletoe pinned to her dress collar, tied with a thin red ribbon. "It looks like mistletoe."

"Yes, it is." She thought of the train conductor, Mr. Blake, and his kind wishes. Wherever he was, she wished him well. And as for the dear friend she'd made on the journey to Montana Territory, she prayed Maeve had found the same kind of unexpected happiness, that God was writing a happy ending for her and her daughter, too.

"Well, if that's mistletoe, you know what we have to do next." Mischief flashed in Cole's blue eyes as he gathered her in his arms. Just the two of them, alone in the vestibule, haloed by lamplight and serenaded by the happy sound of festive conversations ringing in from the sanctuary. He leaned in, his gaze sliding to her mouth. "We have to kiss. It's a rule."

"Not more of your rules," she laughed, already going up on tiptoe.

"From now on," he said, gazing down at her with love. "I have only one rule. I intend to make you the happiest woman ever."

"Too late. I already am." She rested her hand on his chest, felt the thud of his heartbeat, slow and sure. "Merry Christmas, Cole."

"Merry Christmas, my love." He cradled her face in his large, strong hands and kissed her.

Her pulse went still as their lips met. His kiss was pure sweetness, the kind of fairy-tale kiss that promised happily-ever-afters and love everlasting. When it ended, she had tears in her eyes and forever in her heart.

* * * * *

Dear Reader,

Welcome back to my third novella with fellow author and good friend, Janet Tronstad. We had such a great time writing our previous mail-order-bride stories, how could we not do it one more time? We met in Missoula, Montana, on a sunny September day to discuss, brainstorm and create the ideas for our stories. What a fun time we had! Once again, our heroines meet on the westbound train and become friends while riding the rails, wondering how their lives will turn out as mail-order brides. My heroine, Mercy, has decided to accept a convenient marriage, one without the chance of love because of her young son, George. He wants a father so badly and Cole Matheson, her husband-to-be, is very much looking forward to having a son. The problem? Cole has no heart to give her, for his has been shattered by grief. Can happily-ever-after prevail? I hope you enjoy this Christmas tale where God's love heals.

Thank you for choosing *Christmas Hearts.*

Wishing you peace, joy and love this holiday season,

Jillian Hart

Questions for Discussion

1. What was your first impression of Cole? How would you describe him? What do you like most about his character?

2. How would you describe Mercy and Cole's first meeting? What did you learn about her character? What makes you care for Cole?

3. What do you feel for Amelia? What do you like most about her? What do you feel for George? What do you like most about him?

4. When did you know for sure that God meant for Mercy to be Amelia's mother? That she and Cole are meant to be together?

5. What is the story's predominant imagery? How does it contribute to the meaning of the story? Of the romance?

6. Do you see God at work in this story? What meanings do you find there?

7. How would you describe Mercy's faith? Cole's faith?

8. What do you think Mercy and Cole have each learned about love?

MISTLETOE KISS IN DRY CREEK

Janet Tronstad

I am grateful for the many who prayed for my sister,
Margaret, when she was ill with cancer. She is now
dancing in heaven with Jesus, but your prayers
made her feel so loved here on earth. Thank you.

Be not forgetful to entertain strangers, for thereby some have entertained angels unawares.

—*Hebrews* 13:2

Chapter One

Montana Territory
December 20, 1886

With her wool shawl wrapped tight around her shoulders, Maeve Flanagan stepped off the passenger car onto the railroad platform in Miles City and stopped suddenly. She and her four-year-old daughter, Violet, had watched the swirling snow as the train rolled west last night before finally entering the desolate prairie of the Montana Territory. Watching the storm this morning hadn't prepared her for the icy wind that hit her face when she climbed down to the platform, though. It was worse than any gale off the bay in Boston. She lifted the shawl to warm her cheeks. Maybe she had been a fool, trying to escape her past by traveling so far from home to marry a stranger.

Putting her hand over her stomach in an unconscious effort to shield the life that grew within her, she reminded herself that she'd had no other choice. She'd feel better when she met Noah Miller and stood in front of a preacher with him.

Of course, he might refuse to marry her when he found out about the baby.

She hadn't known for sure that she was increasing until the week she received the train tickets. It seemed indelicate to inform Noah of her condition by telegram, especially when she might be wrong. Besides, she wanted him to have time to be charmed by Violet before she said anything. If he liked one child, he'd probably be agreeable to another. She did not know what she'd do if he didn't want them. Infant or no infant, she had nothing left in Boston.

Maeve put a hand up to keep her hat on her head before doing her best to look around. She'd tell Noah of the baby as soon as she could and certainly before they said their vows. He knew she was a recent widow; the baby brought no shame to her. Searching the area, she saw that two rows of painted wood buildings lined the main street of this frontier town. Directly across from her, the Broadwater, Bubble and Company Mercantile had an imposing sign that was visible even in this storm.

Snow had partially turned to hail and caused the few people standing on the store walkways to move inside. Those on the railroad platform huddled together in small groups. The sounds of the horses and wagons that were being driven on the street in front of them gave a faint rhythm to the steady howl of the wind. Maeve didn't see any man standing by himself so Noah must not be here to meet them.

Maeve shivered before turning to the opening behind her and used both hands to reach for her daughter. The train had been early, she assured herself. Noah would be here soon. She would not allow herself to think of any other possibility.

"Cover your head, sweetie." She took the shawl off her shoulders and wrapped it around Violet. The child's thin coat wouldn't keep her warm in the wind. Maeve then swung the girl off the train and moved them both to the side so the next person could exit.

Ash and cinders from the train's smokestack fell with the hail. Maeve kept her arm around her daughter as she looked around the platform more intently. Violet was snug under the shawl, but Maeve's gray wool dress, while her best and the only one made for this kind of weather, did not do much to stop the cold. She couldn't stand out here in the wind for long.

She searched the area again, trying not to worry. When Noah had sent for her, she had wept in relief. She had left her rented room in Boston the day her money had run out and boarded the train to arrive here. God was giving her a second chance. She had begun to wonder if He had abandoned her forever.

Now, she carried a copy of Noah's ad in her Bible.

The ad read: *Passable cook wanted as wife to Montana Territory rancher. Marriage in name only. Must be able to serve up three meals a day for ten to twenty cowboys. Mature widow preferred. Rail fare provided. Separate quarters.*

Maeve wouldn't recognize Noah if he was standing in front of her. He had told her he lived near Dry Creek, a growing ranch area some distance from Miles City. But hadn't said anything about his appearance in the one letter he'd written after she answered his ad. Every man she knew bragged about himself, and Noah's silence in the matter had given her pause. He was probably short and portly. She had wondered about him offering separate quarters until she realized he might be hideously disfigured and wanted his privacy.

No matter, Maeve had told herself firmly at the time. For all that she was only twenty-five-years old, she was long past girlish dreams. She didn't need her pulse to quicken with romance at the sight of her husband. She needed a home for her family. As long as Noah was a good man, they would get along.

Suddenly, Maeve noticed that the wind wasn't blowing. She turned and saw a man standing behind her with a blanket spread high in his extended arms to stop the onslaught of hail. She was tall at nearly six feet, but this man stood at least three inches higher. He was fit, too. His legs were firmly braced on the wooden platform as he stood against the wind with the blanket flapping behind him.

"Flanagan?" the man demanded to know. Snow and pebbles of ice covered the brim of his Stetson hat, but she could tell from his beard that his hair was dark. His eyes were moss-green and seemed steady. Not friendly exactly, but not stern, either.

Maeve nodded as her heart raced. He was neither old nor short. From what she could see of it, his face was strong and probably appealing under his whiskers. Her friend Mercy Jacobs, with whom she'd traveled on the train, had warned her that men in the West were not as refined as those back East, but the man standing in front of her was close to perfect. He might have a beard, but it was trimmed. He didn't need to place an ad asking for a wife. Surely women around here would line up to be courted by this man.

Before she could say anything, the man brought the blanket down over her shoulders and Maeve realized how very cold she had been, standing there shivering. She needed to take better care of herself now that she knew about the baby.

Just then another strong gust of wind hit her, threatening once again to dislodge the old black wool hat she'd securely pinned over her copper hair. She didn't have a chance to put her hand up before the man took the blanket from her shoulders and draped it over her head, hat and all.

"There," he said as though he'd accomplished

something. "We better get going before this storm gets any worse. I need to get back to the ranch and we have to stop by the mercantile and then the church."

He took her arm and looked ready to walk away.

"But—" Maeve burst out and stepped back. The blanket kept her face in shadows and she couldn't see well. "Violet."

The cover shifted as she turned and, through the opening around her face, she saw his bewildered expression. Maeve had answered a half dozen other ads and none of the men wanted a woman with a daughter. A healthy son could be of some help, they had all said, but not a daughter. She hadn't known she was pregnant when she answered those ads so she hadn't mentioned a baby, but when it came time to answer Noah's ad she had simply said she had one child.

He had not asked whether it was a boy or girl or how old the child was; he had just sent two train tickets. At the time, she had thought the man was tolerant and willing to accept any child.

"My daughter," Maeve added as she bent over to tuck her shawl more firmly around Violet. Now that she was here it felt unseemly to mention the babe growing inside her until she and Noah had looked each other in the eyes and smiled in acknowledgment of the bond they were contemplating.

"Oh," Noah said as though he'd forgotten she even had family.

"She won't be any trouble," Maeve said quietly as

she drew the girl closer to her and stepped even with Noah. She was beginning to realize that he had not been kind earlier but, instead, indifferent. She felt a chill go through her that had nothing to do with the storm. She adjusted the blanket, but kept it wrapped around her head. She wished he looked less handsome and more welcoming.

Violet pulled away slightly and Maeve thought it was because the girl sensed her own growing dismay over the man. But then her daughter turned and pointed at something behind them.

Maeve followed Violet's finger. Mercy and her son were knocking on the train window to get their attention. They were on their way farther west to Angel Falls, where Mercy's future husband waited for them.

"My friend," Maeve said by way of explanation to Noah as she lifted her arm in a wave. She and Mercy had said their farewells on the train and Maeve hadn't expected a chance to do so again. They'd promised to write, but she was glad to see her friend's face.

"We don't have time," Noah said impatiently.

"Go-odbye," Violet stuttered as she whispered and waved shyly.

Maeve stood up straighter. Her daughter's trouble with speaking, like the nightmares, had started after seeing her father stabbed to death. Her late husband had taken Violet to some waterfront bar, telling her to stay in the corner, and then he'd sat down and proceeded to be inappropriate with a young lady whose irate father had found them and confronted him. The two men had fought, a full brawl breaking out that had involved the other patrons, and it had all ended badly for her husband. Maeve grieved that he had died, but a larger part of her blamed him for making her a widow.

The train had started rolling again, and Maeve gave another wave and smile to Mercy. When her friend was out of sight, she turned back to Noah.

"Ready?" he asked. He didn't wait for a response, but started moving toward the steps that led down from the railroad platform.

Maeve gathered Violet closer and hurried to follow him.

Just then a young woman ran past them and into the arms of a man standing on the far side of the platform. His whoop of joy made it clear he'd been expecting her. He even took the woman in his arms and kissed her.

Violet stopped and stared at them. "Is she a bride, too?"

"I don't know," Maeve said, her lips pressed together, wondering how she was going to explain to her daughter that not all marriages were filled with happiness.

She had tried to stop the conductor on the train from talking about how wonderful it was going to be when she and Mercy met their respective husbands-to-be. The conductor had even brought by sprigs of mistletoe for the two mail-order brides. He'd said the mistletoe was for their first kisses on Christmas Day with their new husbands.

Maeve looked at Noah out of the corner of her eyes. He didn't look as if a green sprig would tempt him to kiss anyone. His face was as foreboding as the storm clouds. He'd stomped down the wooden steps and stood on the snow-covered street, looking toward the west.

"Is something wrong?" she asked.

If he was troubled about something, then she didn't want to approach him about the baby.

"Just that we're late," he said as he turned to her. "The clouds coming in look worse. And now the clerk in the mercantile should be coming back from his noon meal and I don't see him."

"Oh, well, that's—" Maeve stopped. He had a frown on his face, but he didn't appear overly angry. If she didn't tell him now, when would she?

She took a deep breath and glanced down because she couldn't bear to watch his eyes as she said what she had to say. "Maybe he has a baby at home and is taking a moment to rock the wee thing. The little ones can be sweet, don't you think? Makes us all wish we had one."

She realized she had to see him to judge his reaction so she looked up at him.

"He's not married," Noah responded as he stood there, his eyes bland as they watched hers curiously.

"Oh." She looked at his eyes and waited a moment longer.

His green eyes didn't darken even with the clouds overhead. He showed no sudden spark of understanding.

Finally, his eyes broke away from hers.

"The clerk's life is his own that way," Noah mused idly as he stared down the street again. "No one to answer to."

He sounded as if he envied the man. Maeve didn't know what to say to that, but she apparently didn't need to say anything as her future husband continued on.

"Of course, he's not responsible for taking care of a bunkhouse of men so he might not understand how important it is for us to get our order in for supplies."

"Working men need to eat," Maeve agreed cautiously. Noah had been clear that he wanted a cook for a wife. She kept trying not to let that dismay her. Many marriages started out with less. She wished he had smiled at the thought of babies, though.

Noah gestured across the street to the general store. "We'll have to hurry. We don't have time to do much looking around. As it is, I'll have to ask the boy who works there to bring most of what we order out in his wagon after the storm. And the preacher will be at the church soon."

With that, Noah turned and held out a hand to help her down the steps. Then he gestured as if to lift Violet down to the street, but Maeve said she'd do it. Once she had her daughter next to her, she pulled the girl close and faced them both in the right direction.

As they walked across the snow-covered street, Maeve convinced herself there was something reassuring about the man. He might not be friendly, but he was clearly used to taking care of others. Besides, his gruffness would likely go away when he got to know her and Violet better.

She hoped she was right as she pushed back her fears.

Maeve felt the wind stop again as Noah stepped up onto a wooden walk that was in front of the mercantile. He stomped the snow off his boots.

Frost outlined the window that looked into the establishment. Various items were right inside on a table. Maeve's breath caught when she saw a doll in a red dress lying near a flowered teapot.

Oh, no, Christmas Eve, she thought. She'd almost forgotten the holiday and it was four days from now.

She had no money for presents, not even for Violet. The girl had wanted a doll like the one in the window ever since she'd been able to crawl. Months ago, Maeve had decided her daughter would finally have her wish this Christmas. Her husband had been making money—he'd told her he'd gotten some work at the waterfront—and Maeve had been putting in extra hours as a scrubwoman.

She almost had enough saved up for a doll when everything turned upside down. She'd been fired from her job because the lady of the house didn't want "that man's widow" working for her any longer, even though all Maeve ever did was scrub the floors and do the heavy washing. She was given no references when she was told to leave. She'd finally bought a newspaper and read the awful things people were saying about her late husband. And about her.

People said that she had known about her husband's scheme to seduce rich young women and then threaten to expose them unless their families offered up a fair amount of money. The reporters even speculated that she had some of that money left and creditors came to her door demanding payment on her late husband's debts. They showed her papers he had signed for gambling debts and she'd been unable to pay them. She didn't know what her husband had done with the money he'd forced from the families. Likely, he had gambled it away. The only thing he had ever given her was the odd coin here and there that he added to their savings for the doll.

They'd been destitute when Noah's letter had come with the train tickets.

"Pretty," Violet whispered and pointed. The doll had auburn hair and blue eyes like hers. "What's her name, Mommy?"

The blanket no longer kept the cold away. Maeve shivered, but she noticed Violet didn't hesitate in her speech at all, not when talking about the doll.

"Hush now," Maeve said quietly. "The doll doesn't have a name."

"Oh." Violet breathed in dismay. "Doesn't she have a daddy to love her?"

Maeve almost broke down. As unfaithful as her husband had been, he'd always charmed their daughter. He told her he'd named her for his favorite flower, the most delicate, beautiful blooming plant in the whole world. The truth was, Maeve had discovered at his graveside, Violet had been the name of one of his several lovers. He must have thought it was quite the joke to name their daughter after a woman he had been free with since before he married Maeve.

"The doll doesn't care about love," Maeve told the girl, her words more harsh than she intended. Her heart had been broken all over again when her husband's lover had confronted her that day, demanding to have a token of him for a remembrance, preferably something with a precious stone that she could pawn.

Maeve forced her face to relax and smiled reassuringly at her daughter.

Violet didn't look convinced, but she didn't say anything more.

Maeve looked over at Noah, hoping he hadn't been listening. He was reaching for the doorknob and didn't seem to have been paying any attention to them. She was relieved.

"Maybe they'll still have a doll like that next Christmas," Maeve whispered finally, softening her voice and offering her daughter what hope she could. The girl nodded solemnly and Maeve resolved to put together a sock doll for Violet for Christmas. It wouldn't be the beauty in the window, but her daughter would have something to hug as she went to sleep at night.

Noah stomped the snow off his boots as he opened the wide door leading into the mercantile. It was darker than usual inside because of the coming storm, but it was warm. The place smelled of coffee, and he saw a new barrel of pickles sitting on the floor by the counter. Bright bolts of cloth were on a shelf to his right. Cans of peaches and bags of dried beans were to his left.

Noah watched to be sure the woman and girl made it through the door. He had yet to even see the Flanagan woman's face since she kept the blanket hooded over it. His impression of her on the railroad platform was of a tall drab woman with an awful hat pulled down to cover her ears. From what he could tell, she was thin. He hoped she was up to cooking for his crew. His men knew how to drive cattle and they were loyal, but there had been grumbling in the bunkhouse about the burnt biscuits and tough meat the ranch had served up for the past two years. Last fall, he'd ordered one of the cowboys, Dakota, to take over feeding the men. The cowboy hadn't been much of a cook and he was anxious to have the duty taken away from him.

The men would give anyone who didn't feed them better than Dakota a hard time. It was worse in the winter when they spent half of their time in the bunkhouse dreaming of donuts and pies—the kind of delicacies, they said, that required a woman's hand to make properly.

He suspected it was all the idle time that had caused his men to come to him with the idea of placing an ad for a female cook. He told them there was no point. Women were so scarce in the Montana Territory that no woman would stay longer than a couple of weeks before she got married and left. They knew that as well as he did, but Dakota refused to accept it. He said he was going to find a way to get a cook who would stay.

The next thing Noah knew, he'd received a letter from a woman who had answered the ad Dakota and the men had put in a newspaper asking for a mail-order bride—for him. He'd demanded to see the ad and the ranch hands had given him a copy. He had been glad to see Dakota had some sense and had indicated the marriage would be in name only. Then he'd wondered if an older widow might just be interested in the kind of an arrangement his men had proposed. He checked the dates and saw that the ad had run for a full month and a half before he received even that one reply. He figured that meant there had been no confusion about the offer being made. Most women had discarded it.

Noah had intended to throw the letter he received away, but it had sat on his bedside table for two weeks. Every night he'd read it and tried to write some words to tell the woman there had been a misunderstanding. He'd had one wife and had no intentions of ever seeking another.

But the sparse words on the plain piece of paper had haunted him. He could almost feel the woman's desperation as she penned the few words telling him that she was an immigrant from Northern Ireland, a mature widow who had worked as a scrubwoman until her husband had been killed and she'd lost her job. She had no other family and was looking for a home for herself and her child. She had taken lessons to improve her speech, she said, and she knew also how to sew. Maybe it was the lack of polish and detail that had spoken to him. He'd known discouragement so deep it threatened the soul. He'd sensed this woman had nothing but a fragile pride stopping her from begging for help.

Finally, one night he'd written to her, telling her to come if she hadn't already found another position. And he'd prayed that she had. He had repeated that he had separate quarters for her, hoping to assure her that he didn't mean to take advantage of her plight. Once she had saved some money, he would offer to have the marriage annulled if she wanted. He knew how easily women, especially immigrants, starved to death in cities like Boston after they lost their husbands and their jobs.

"I mean to pay you," Noah said as he turned around to speak to the woman. "They didn't mention that in the ad, but—"

She wasn't there. She hadn't followed him over to the counter like he had assumed. Instead, she was bent over the little girl, speaking in a low voice. All he saw was the top of her blanketed head, but something about her and the child made him uneasy. She hadn't mentioned her age in the brief letter she'd written, but mature surely meant someone old enough to be a grandmother. He was thirty-three and he figured someone of that description had to be in her fifties. But not many women that age would have a young child.

The girl was probably her granddaughter, he told himself in relief. Maybe she thought he would frown upon her bringing a child who wasn't hers.

Just then Jimmy, the boy who ran errands in the store, came out from the back room.

"Help you?" He nodded in greeting. "I got some of your order in the wagon. I left room for a couple of trunks. But I got in the ham you wanted and a side of bacon. I'll bring the rest out later."

"My wife is going to put in a full order for that later delivery, but you'll need to pick up her trunk from the railroad station now," Noah said loudly enough for the woman to hear. "Flanagan is the name."

His words got her attention and she turned away from the display and started walking closer to him. He couldn't see anything on that table to appeal to a woman unless it was the china teapot.

"Put the pot in the window in our wagon, too," Noah whispered as he leaned in and spoke quietly to Jimmy. "Wrap it in a sack and see if you can find some red ribbon to go around it, too."

Noah was pleased with himself. He hadn't bought anyone a Christmas present since his wife ran away over two years ago. Oh, he always gave the ranch hands a twenty-dollar gold piece each. But a woman liked a gift.

"I'm sure you know what to stock for supplies in the kitchen," Noah said once the woman reached him. "Just tell Jimmy here. He can write it down."

"I don't know." She sounded a little alarmed.

The wind had made it hard to hear her earlier, but inside here he caught a hint of gentle Irish brogue in her voice. He liked it.

"They have almost everything you'd want in the mercantile here," he assured her.

She was silent for a moment.

"I'll just get your usual order," she finally said,

sounding hesitant. "Until I've had a chance to check on what spices you have and everything."

Noah frowned. "There's not much on the shelves. We haven't had a cook on the place since my wife left two years ago."

"Your wife?" The woman looked up at that, no longer timid in her tone. If the sky outside wasn't going dark, he would have been able to see her face fully. He was sure there'd be some spark there, but the shadows hid her.

"She divorced me." He didn't like talking about his wife, but the woman deserved to know his past, especially since he'd brought it up. "She didn't think I could give her enough fancy things—you know, clothes and furniture. Things like that."

Flanagan didn't say anything and he was grateful for her tact.

"She wasn't much of a cook," he added. "Could barely make pancakes. Either raw in the middle or so thin there was nothing to them. But she did order in spices and tins of oysters."

He supposed it was during his marriage that he had become accustomed to poor cooking. His wife had had visions of entertaining visiting dignitaries, but he didn't know any such people so the few imported tins gathered dust on the shelves. He'd been so miserable during that time, he hadn't cared about eating and his men, maybe sensing how bad things were between him and his wife, hadn't complained much about the food, either.

Noah turned to the boy behind the counter. "Add a few cases of canned peaches to the order." He figured his men deserved something festive to eat. And maybe their ad would work out better than he'd expected. "Put the peaches in the wagon. I think there'll be room since there's only one trunk."

"Oh, and tell the clerk when he gets back that he'll be taking his supply orders from my wife from now on," he added with a nod to Maeve.

Jimmy looked between him and the woman and nodded solemnly. "Yes, sir."

Noah suddenly realized the youngster had learned more about him in the past few minutes than most adults in town had learned in the decade he'd lived here.

"Well, we best get going," Noah said as he turned to the woman. "The church is only a few doors down."

"I'd like to talk to you before we see the preacher," she said then, her voice low and serious.

Noah felt his heart sink. He feared she was going to back out. Although why she would, he wasn't certain. She hadn't seen much of the country around here. His wife had always said the mercantile wasn't as well stocked as stores back East, but that seemed a small reason to leave. It might be the weather, though. Some people couldn't tolerate the bad storms they had here, especially if they found themselves snowbound. But she was Irish. And from Boston. Shouldn't she be used to the cold?

Noah looked around. There were no private places in the mercantile and he didn't want his business spread all over the territory. If he was going to be left at the altar, he didn't want everyone to know. The divorce had done enough damage to his pride.

"We can take a moment in the church," he said finally.

The woman nodded and took the hand of the girl.

They walked to the door.

"The preacher is expecting us," he added as he stepped over to open the door. "So he'll be there when we arrive."

He turned back to Jimmy. "You'll have to finish loading the supplies in the wagon. Remember the peaches."

A knowing twinkle appeared in the boy's eyes. "I'll get them there. And congratulations."

Noah frowned, but nodded his thanks. He supposed it was impossible to keep the wedding plans a secret even if the woman backed out. The ranch hands had probably already announced it to everyone they'd seen in the days since he'd told them Maeve had boarded the train in Boston and was heading south to pick up the rail line that would bring her west.

Noah reached over and opened the doors.

"Just follow me," he said to the woman as he stepped out to the street.

The wind hit him and he hunched his shoulders. He was a God-fearing man and he didn't believe in superstitions, but he wondered if it was wise to get married with a snowstorm brewing. His first wife would have been calling the whole thing off by now. Maybe the widow was wise to have second thoughts.

Chapter Two

Tiny hailstones were still falling as Maeve followed Noah out of the mercantile. The damp cold hit her face and she reached down to scoop Violet into her arms. She wrapped the blanket around both of them, even though she could barely carry her daughter.

A huge amount of snow covered the walkway. Maeve had worn her best leather shoes and didn't want to ruin them so she began to gingerly place her feet in the trail of footsteps Noah had left behind. These were her church shoes, and, before she left Boston, she had promised Violet that they could go to church when they got settled here. She didn't want anyone to look down on her and Violet so she'd need the shoes. The church people in Boston had been very particular about what a woman wore on her feet and on her head. That was even before they'd rejected her on account of her late husband.

Maeve had taken only two steps when Noah turned around. The clouds had darkened since they'd gone into the mercantile. He had his Stetson firmly pulled down on his head, but his beard was whiter in the snow.

"Here," he said as he held out his arms. "I can carry her."

"I don't know." Ever since the stabbing of her father, Violet had been skittish around men. They scared her. Maeve didn't know how to explain all of that to Noah, though, especially not standing in the freezing wind in the middle of the walkway. "She's content under the blanket."

"She'll still have the shawl if I take her," Noah said.

Maeve hesitated, but she supposed the girl needed to get used to Noah at some point.

She bent down to whisper to her daughter. "The man's going to carry you so you're out of the cold faster. Is that all right?"

It was a moment before she felt her daughter nod her head slightly.

"Thank you," Maeve said as she held her daughter out.

Noah took the girl and kept walking down the street. Now that Maeve was free to pick up her skirts, she stepped a lot faster behind him. She didn't want to be too far away from him in case Violet needed her.

Noah waited for her in front of the small white

church. She liked it. There was no formal steeple like they had back East. The place looked almost friendly and she saw smoke coming from a chimney in the back. The windows on each side were small and rimmed with frost. She doubted they had been pushed open since the last day of fall. Snow had blown against the casings and collected all around. She believed this church would not turn a woman away because of her husband's sins.

After she arrived at the church steps, she looked at Noah. "I'll need a few minutes to talk to you."

He nodded as he opened the door and gestured for her to go inside ahead of him.

The smell of burning wood greeted her as she walked into the church. The blanket, while still wrapped around her head as best as she could manage, was cold and damp as she stood there. Some of the snowflakes on the wool must have melted while they were in the mercantile. Now a musty scent was beginning to rise from the covering as the heat become more pronounced.

It was dark enough inside the church that her eyes needed to adjust. A cast-iron heating stove stood in the far corner next to a pulpit. That was where the heat was coming from. Student desks were pushed against the sides of the church and, she noticed, there was a blackboard in the front of the room. A faint gray line on the floor, which looked as if it had endured many scrubbings, divided the room. This was

Saturday and benches were lined up in the room now. She'd heard these frontier churches often used the same building for a schoolhouse and a church.

Maeve relaxed her grip on the blanket wrapped around her head and felt it fall to her shoulders. As the wool slid off her head, it took her hat with it.

She felt a moment's unease. Her thick, riotous copper hair had given her trouble in the church she'd attended back East. People seemed to think a woman kept her morals in her hair knot and strands of hers were always coming loose. And that was before her husband had been loudly denounced from the pulpits in Boston. Maeve hadn't trusted the clergy since then. It was the ministers who had turned her employer against her.

"Welcome." A man's voice came from the front of the room and she saw a figure rise from a chair next to the stove. Tall and dressed in black, the white-haired man swayed a little as he walked. "I'm Reverend Olson. I've been expecting the two of you."

She blinked the last of the snowflakes off her eyelids and saw him lean on his cane with one hand as he walked down the side of the benches with the other hand outstretched.

"Excuse me, I should have said the three of you," he added as he smiled at Violet even though the child had her face pressed against Noah's chest and couldn't even see the reverend.

"My wife is going to be here any minute," the

preacher continued, beaming at them all now. "She'll bring our neighbor Mrs. Barker with her so you have the witnesses you need for a legal marriage certificate."

"I need to discuss something with Noah first," Maeve said. She couldn't marry him without telling him about the baby.

Then she heard a choking sound behind her and turned.

Noah was staring at her. "Your hair."

Maeve squared her shoulder. If the man had something against red hair, he should have mentioned it earlier.

"I told you I was from Northern Ireland," she told him defiantly. "Everyone knows a lot of women in that part of the country have hair like this. I can't change the color. I've been working to tame my voice so it sounds American, but there's no changing my hair."

Maeve knew she should back down. This man held her future. If he was going to reject her because of her hair, he certainly wouldn't accept her with a baby.

She'd forgotten Reverend Olson had been talking until she saw that he was waiting patiently at the end of the row of benches. He'd given up on shaking anyone's hand, but he was watching Noah and her with some interest.

"You haven't changed your voice as much as you

think," Noah finally said as he sat Violet down on a bench.

Maeve glared at him. "I've done my best."

"There's music when you speak," Noah said, his voice clipped as if he was angry, even though she didn't know why he would be. He had removed his hat and set it down by her daughter. He ran his hand through his damp strands of hair.

"I like to sing," Maeve said defiantly. She looked into the man's eyes. The color had darkened and they were almost dark brown instead of green. She didn't know why she fought when she was afraid, but everything in her seemed to lead her that way.

Noah nodded as he studied her some more, obviously trying to decide something.

"I suppose I could put blackening in my hair if the red color bothers you that much," Maeve forced herself to say. She couldn't stand against the man's wishes. Not when she remembered how destitute she was. How would she care for a baby and her daughter? She glanced over at Violet and saw the girl was watching both of them intently. She'd sacrifice anything to give her children a decent life, even her pride.

Noah shook his head. "Your hair is magnificent. Like the sun in a red sky at night."

He didn't say it as if it was a good thing, but Maeve was still relieved. She wasn't sure she could walk around with blackening on her head.

"It's just I thought you were a widow," Noah said, his voice tinged with reproach.

Maeve felt her heart beat faster. "Who would lie about being a widow? My husband died seven weeks ago. You can read any of the Boston papers if you don't believe me. They certainly covered his death long enough."

Everyone was silent for a moment. Maeve could hear the crackle of the fire and noticed the preacher had left the door to the stove open, no doubt to warm the room faster. It reminded her that the coal bin for the small fireplace in her rented room would have been empty by now, regardless of whether she had been able to leave or not. She'd burned only enough coal to keep them from freezing. She couldn't take her children back to that life; they might not survive next time.

"You're too young for the kind of marriage I have in mind," Noah finally said. "That's why I asked for a mature widow." He looked at her, and this time he didn't bother to hide his reproach. "Why, you're scarcely old enough to be a wife, let alone a widow."

"I'm twenty-five-years old," Maeve said as she straightened her back so she was her full height. She was tall enough to intimidate most men, but she didn't seem to move Noah. "Old enough to have a daughter and lose a husband in a very public and humiliating fashion."

Noah was quiet. "I'm sorry."

She wasn't ready to mention the baby. Not in anger like this.

They were both quiet for a moment.

"I'm sure you've had some hard times," he finally added, "but life can change. You're young enough to find a happy marriage. You're not who I expected."

Maeve had traveled over two thousand miles, breathing the smoke of the train and pretending to be grateful for the stale butter sandwiches, the only food she'd had to pack with them when they'd left. Her daughter was suffering from bad memories; it was almost Christmas; and before long, Maeve would likely have bouts of morning sickness.

"Violet and I might not be the kind of people you expected," Maeve said, her voice growing strong. "But we are who you got."

Noah looked a little stunned at the force in her voice and she had to admit she was surprised herself. But she was at the end of her road. She didn't have money to wait for another mail-order husband. Not that she was likely to find one now that she'd have a baby to consider as well as Violet. Besides, she thought indignantly, Noah shouldn't have put an ad in the newspaper unless he expected someone to answer it.

Maeve looked over at the reverend.

"I just need to discuss something with Noah," she said. "If you'll excuse us."

She willed her nerves to stop racing around in her stomach.

The preacher nodded as a couple of middle-aged women came through the door, brushing snow and hail off their garments.

“My wife,” the reverend gestured to a plump, kindly looking woman.

Then he introduced the other woman, who had dark hair and a stern face. “Mrs. Barker.”

“Pleased to meet you both,” Maeve said with a smile for the women. They nodded in return.

Maeve reached up to her hair. Curls sprang from her head the way they did in damp weather. The whole bunch of it had escaped its pins and was, no doubt, spreading out around her head like a wild dandelion on fire. She looked down and saw her hat had rolled under one of the benches. She walked over and bent down to retrieve it. The cook at the house where she had worked had given her that old wool hat so she could take Violet to church without having anyone gossip or complain that she wasn’t dressed in the right church clothes.

When she stood up, she saw that Noah had walked close to her.

“I don’t mean for our marriage to be real,” he said to her. He spoke low, clearly not wanting the others to hear. “If that’s what you want to talk about, don’t worry. I thought the ad made it clear that I’m suggesting we have one of those—what do they call them—marriages in name only?"

"I read the ad. I know you don't want a regular marriage."

She meant to keep her voice quiet, but she was troubled. What kind of a wedded life would they have? No affection. And no more children after the baby that was coming—which he didn't even know about she realized with a sinking heart. Maybe he didn't want more children.

Maeve barely noticed the gasps of the two older women. She was watching the deep red spread over Noah's face.

"I thought you'd be fifty years old at least," he protested, no longer trying to be quiet. "A marriage in name only means sleeping apart."

"I know what it means," Maeve snapped.

Noah's jaw was clenched and his words came out low. "You're too young to give up your life for a steady job. I'm trying to give you a chance to avoid this marriage. If it's a matter of money to get home, I can give you some—with extra."

"I don't take charity," Maeve said defiantly, even though it wasn't true. After she'd lost her job, she wouldn't have been able to provide food for her and Violet if her only friend, the cook at the house where she used to work, hadn't given her bags of foodstuffs every few days. Her pride had been another recent casualty in her life.

"Good, then work for me," Noah challenged her. "You and your daughter can live in the house. I'll move to the bunkhouse."

Someone gasped even louder than before and Maeve heard footsteps coming closer.

When Maeve looked up, she saw the stern-faced woman, Mrs. Barker, standing there with her hands on her hips as she scolded Noah. "You can't ask this young woman to live out there with all those ranch hands of yours and no wedding ring on her finger. Shame on you, Noah Miller. You know her reputation will be in tatters if she does that."

"I don't mind," Maeve said quietly. A reputation was a luxury she could not afford to consider.

"She and her girl would be staying in my room in the house," Noah assured the other woman. "My men will vouch for me staying in that room off the bunkhouse. You don't need to worry about Maeve and her girl. I've got a comfortable bed for them. Made the frame myself."

"I can't take your bed." Maeve blushed when she said it. Sleeping in the man's bed felt intimate. She glanced around and saw that the preacher was walking toward them now, too.

"Yes, you can." Noah's voice was deep and filled with some emotion she couldn't identify. He'd turned from the other woman and was focusing on her. "It comes with the job. You'll need to rest if you expect to get up early and fix breakfast for the men. Coffee and fried eggs will do. Can you cook them?"

"Anyone can fry an egg," Maeve said, feeling relief flow over her. He meant to keep her for now. "And, coffee, of course."

"We're set, then?" he asked.

She gave him a nod as she felt a slight roll in her stomach. It must have been the thought of frying eggs. The smell had given her problems when she was carrying Violet, too. Not that she had a choice now. She had to cook eggs.

Her friend in Boston had said that ad might not be all she hoped and it looked as if she was right. But it was winter and she had a daughter as well as a baby to consider. She needed to keep them warm and fed. Besides, if she gave Noah time to come to love Violet, she could tell him about the baby.

Noah clenched his hands into a fist. The woman looked pale. He had confused things and he didn't know how to make everything right. After she got rid of that hat, the woman had been glorious, with her pink cheeks and her copper hair tumbling down to her shoulders. She was a beauty and deserved the kind of happiness he'd heard a good marriage could bring. The very thought of working for him seemed to turn her sickly, though.

It depressed him to have to disappoint her, but he hadn't been able to keep his first wife, Allison, happy. And he'd loved her. Her list of things she wanted had been long—a proper house, a set of English china, a silk dress for every day of the week, copper pans in the kitchen, Irish linens in the bedroom, hand-painted angels on the mantel in the parlor and a maid. He would have sold every possession he had if she would have stayed with him and raised a family. Unfortunately, he hadn't had much worth selling in those days.

The irony was that, after she'd left him, his herd of cattle had increased. Slowly, he'd built up his ranch, adding the kind of proper house Allison had always said she wanted. He never expected to see her again, but he'd found himself adding all of the little luxuries she had wanted. It was more to prove to himself that he could afford them than because he had much use for them.

Maeve was silent and the preacher was standing next to her.

"I can't take advantage of her," Noah said to the reverend, feeling guilty now that Maeve had stopped being angry with him. "And that's what I would be doing. She deserves a better marriage and she'll find it if she takes some time."

"I won't be changing my mind," Maeve said.

"You can get married any day you want if that's what you decide to do," the preacher announced calmly. "Things might look different in the morning. Better to put it off until you are both happy about the decision. Your men will make good chaperones. I'll speak to them."

Noah noticed that Maeve was watching him.

"Sounds sensible to me," Noah said, ignoring that spark within him. He had begun to wonder what it would be like to forget about fairness and marry the woman. He had little doubt, though, that Maeve would find a better husband than him if she took some time to look around. The new banker was a widower. He was a few years older than Noah, but he seemed nice enough. And he played the violin. Women liked things like that.

"As long as I get paid for the cooking I do," Maeve said, her voice wavering a little as though someone had taken advantage of her in the past.

She suddenly looked even younger than her twenty-five years, and he felt his hands curl into fists. He would not mind having a word or two with the man who had given Maeve a hard time. But he couldn't say anything.

So he nodded instead. "We better start heading home, then. Jimmy should have our wagon sitting out back."

It didn't take long to say farewell to the preacher and the two women. They all promised to come back to the church in the next few days if that was what he and Maeve wanted. Noah could tell they were disappointed. He came to hear the sermons when the weather was nice enough to get into town, and he knew the women had been praying for him to find a wife. He hadn't asked them to do that, but he suspected his ranch hands were behind that, too.

The winds didn't let up when Noah helped Maeve and the girl into the wagon. He brought forward a couple of old blankets and a buffalo hide he kept in the back for when the weather was like this. He wrapped a blanket around their heads and tucked the others around their legs. He put the hide over all.

"That'll keep you warm," Noah said as he picked up the reins. When he'd gotten out the blankets, he'd checked to see that the teapot was in the back, hidden behind the cases of canned peaches.

Noah set the horses to their course and they pulled the wagon along the road.

When he drove the team over the rise that led down to his ranch, his face was raw from the force of the blowing snow and the sun was beginning to set behind the storm clouds. If it had been a nicer day, he would have taken pleasure in showing Maeve and the little one the view from the top of the rise. His land stretched out in all directions as far as the eye could see. At this time of year, only the tumbleweeds broke the whiteness on the ground, but in the spring tufts of green grass would dot the landscape.

His two-story house was nestled in a dip after the rise, making it close to the creek that ran through his property. Noah thought sometimes the land he'd chosen for his home was curved until it looked as if God was holding the house in His hands. Noah never mentioned his fanciful thinking to anyone, but he liked to walk up to the rise when he prayed in the mornings. He knew he had many blessings even if the love of a wife wasn't one of them. Some distance from the house was a tall red barn with a long, squat bunkhouse built against its side. The ranch hands never had cause to complain about their quarters. Their long room was snug and homey with a fireplace at each end and chairs scattered around for sitting on a winter evening. Beds lined the walls.

The house itself was the jewel on his property. Windows faced in every direction, each one of them gleaming despite the frost curling around the edges of the glass. He'd had to send back East for the beveled windows in the main door. A wide porch wrapped around the front part of the house and, in the summer, bright red geranium plants were scattered around in clay pots.

Suddenly, Noah frowned. What looked like a sheet was blowing from one of the upstairs windows. Then he noticed that the door to the bunkhouse had opened and a stream of ranch hands was spilling out. They stood a moment, watching the wagon as Noah guided it down the road. Dakota was in the lead, waving his hat as the men started to walk closer.

Noah didn't know whether to warn Maeve that they were being welcomed or try to figure out a hand signal that would convince the ranch hands to go back inside and pretend they hadn't noticed them coming home.

Finally, it was too late to do either.

Maeve had lifted her head out of the blankets and was looking straight ahead.

"Is someone doing the wash?" she asked, puzzled. "Isn't it too cold for anything to dry?"

"It's not laundry," he said and hesitated a few seconds before adding. "It's hung there to celebrate our wedding."

"But we didn't get married," she protested, looking over at him in surprise. "Oh, of course, your men don't know that, do they?"

He shrugged as he looked into her green eyes. The shadows made them dark, but he noticed they had some sparks to them that they hadn't before. The woman was not hiding her feelings from him as much as she had earlier.

"They mean well," he said, smiling at her. "And, if I'm not mistaken, they've already told everyone from miles around that we were getting married today. They've been waiting since I got your letter. But it doesn't matter. I'll explain it to them and they'll spread the word that it didn't happen."

Maeve looked away from him then and his throat tightened. She was upset that they had not gone through with their vows. If he didn't believe she'd feel differently in a couple of days, he would have turned the wagon around and headed back to the church.

But he couldn't live with a woman who felt trapped in a marriage to him. His wife's unhappiness had left them both miserable.

Just then, his men came up close to the wagon. They were all noisy, grinning and carrying their rifles. No doubt they intended to fire off a volley in honor of the occasion. Noah stopped the horses and held up his arm. He wouldn't be surprised if Dakota had organized all of this; that man was determined to give up his cooking duties.

The crew looked at Noah expectantly.

"We're not married yet," he explained as he surveyed the ranch hands. "I felt it was only right to give her a chance to see what she's in for before she goes through with it. In the meantime, I know you'll honor Maeve as if she were my wife."

"Maeve?" one of the men in front of him asked as he tilted his head. "Isn't that Irish?"

"You can call her Mrs. Flanagan for the time being," Noah replied. Some of the men had hard feelings against the Irish after a brawl with some soldiers from nearby Fort Keogh. "She and her daughter, Violet, are my guests. Now let me get this wagon up by the porch. You can help carry everything inside before the storm gets any worse."

He started the horses forward.

"Is she going to cook for us in the morning?"

Dakota called after them. "I mean, since she didn't marry you?"

Noah reined in the horses and looked over at Maeve. She had pushed more of the blankets back so she could see what was happening. Her green eyes were sleepy. Her hair tousled. He didn't need to ask to know she was exhausted.

"Dakota can fry eggs in the morning," Noah said. "Same as usual."

That was enough to make all of the men turn to stare at him.

"But he burnt them last time," one of his men reminded Noah, although he didn't do it loudly. "I almost couldn't eat mine. And you know me. I eat anything."

"I was looking forward to a biscuit," a younger cowboy complained, as well. "How hard can that be to make?"

Dakota bristled at this and turned to the younger man. "I'd like to see you try to make some."

They hadn't had bread of any kind for months. The last batch of biscuits Dakota had made had been hard as stones. No one could eat them. Noah had finally ordered the man to stop even trying so they wouldn't keep wasting flour. He wasn't sure if Dakota was relieved or still held a grudge over the incident.

"The woman deserves a rest," Noah said. And he intended to see that she had one.

He wasn't sure what decision he and Maeve were going to make about the marriage, but he did believe she was a decent woman who had been overcome by trouble. Whether she wanted to marry him or not, he meant to see that she got a new start in life.

"I'll get up early anyway," Maeve said with a yawn and then sat up straighter on the wagon bench. "I always do."

Noah didn't answer as he pulled the horses to a halt in front of the house. For however long Maeve and her daughter were with him, he wanted them to be welcome.

"You're entitled to stay in bed in the morning," he said firmly. "You've had a long trip here. And treat my place like your home. Don't let the ranch hands convince you to get up and cook for them."

Maeve looked at him, speechless, and then smiled before turning to wake up her daughter.

"I can carry her in," Noah said as he started to climb down off his wagon. "I'll come around."

His men had walked up to the back of the wagon and were starting to unload the supplies.

Noah hurried to the other side of the wagon and held out his arms for the girl. He had moved most of his clothes out of the bedroom yesterday and put them in the room at the end of the bunkhouse. The woman and her child would be comfortable in the house. His room shared a wall with the parlor fireplace so it was the warmest place in his house, except for the kitchen.

He could hear Violet murmuring as her mother gathered her up. The girl was likely still half-asleep. Noah's hat was knocked off by the wind and it fell into the back of the wagon. He left it there since the woman was ready to set the girl in his arms. For a moment, he let her weight settle. He was surprised at the contentment he felt holding her. He'd never had a child on his ranch before, not one he could lay claim to as his own. His neighbors, the Hargroves, brought their girls over once in a while when they visited, but there was no one else.

Noah had hoped his wife would have his children, but, even if she had stayed, she had made it clear she didn't intend to be a mother. She had muttered something about little ones having sticky fingers and colic.

The girl shifted suddenly in his arms, and then stiffened as she opened her eyes. A shriek of pure terror split the early night as she screamed.

"What's wrong?" Noah looked up at Maeve in alarm. The girl was rigid in his arms.

"She's frightened." Maeve slid to the end of the wagon bench and opened her arms to take her daughter back. "She was startled when she saw you. I should have known. She hadn't fully woken up yet. I wasn't thinking."

Noah gave the now-shivering girl back to her

mother. Maeve was apologizing, but Noah didn't think she was surprised. The child had been terrified.

Dakota had opened the door to the house and two other ranch hands were moving the trunk inside. They set down the burden and ran back to the wagon at the sound of the scream.

"What's wrong?" Dakota asked breathlessly. The other ranch hands crowded around.

Maeve was rubbing her daughter's back and Violet's whimpering was slowing down.

"We'll be fine," Noah answered. The girl's eyes had opened wider at the sight of the other men. She might be silent now, but she wasn't at ease.

"Give her some room to breathe," Noah advised the other men.

The men were used to animals that panicked and nodded.

"Anything she needs," Dakota whispered as the men turned their backs.

They all walked away quietly and picked up the trunk again.

Noah waited a few minutes for the girl to start breathing normally.

"Let me help you down," he finally said as he lifted his arms up to help the burdened Maeve down. He pulled her toward him and then let her slide to the ground. Carefully, he avoided touching her daughter cradled in her embrace. Something in his heart shifted as he watched Maeve protect the girl. Not all women were so fierce in defending their young. His wife never would have been.

When Maeve stood squarely on the ground, he put his arm around her and escorted her to his house. He could feel her trembling, but he didn't say anything. He sensed she was too proud to admit to being shaken up, though he found he liked having her lean on him.

He wondered how they were going to live with each other, even for the duration of the storm. He had always said that his heart had been torn out by its roots when his wife left. Now he suspected there might have been a seed left behind. He doubted it was enough for him to love someone again, but it might be enough to remind him keenly of all that he was missing. He liked being able to protect the woman and her child. He knew that when they were gone from him he'd worry.

With those despairing thoughts, he reached down and turned the knob so he could open the door to his home. He looked down and saw red strands of hair sticking out around where the blanket was wrapped. Maeve moved farther toward him. He was relieved that it was the situation and not him that made her hesitate.

"It's a good house," he said, pausing with his hand on the doorknob. "Safe and warm. Live in it as your own while you're here."

As he swung the door wide-open so they could all enter, he wondered how long the blizzard would last.

"Your daughter will feel better once she's been here for a while," he said, adding the last bit of comfort he could, wondering what had happened to Maeve and Violet to make the girl so afraid.

Chapter Three

Darkness continued to fall as Maeve let Noah guide her through the main door of the house, down a short hallway and into a large square room that smelled faintly of coffee. She figured he sat here sometimes and drank his morning beverage. The windows were bare and must provide a good view of his ranch as he emptied his cup. Tonight, however, the gray sky outside didn't let in much light. Despite the picture she'd painted in her mind about the man and his coffee, Maeve sensed the room was seldom used and had seen much sadness.

Or maybe it was her, she thought.

"Your home's lovely," she forced herself to say politely, clutching Violet close to her as though she needed to protect the girl. By now, she could see brocade-covered chairs in the shadows so she knew she wasn't in the kitchen. It was the parlor, maybe.

She still didn't look up as she felt drops of melting snow fall from her tumble of hair, landing on the plank floor beneath her.

"I'll wipe up the spots," she said. "We're dripping everywhere."

Noah grunted, but didn't say anything.

She didn't blame him. If only Violet had been able to hide her fears, he might have come to see her daughter's delightful side. As it was, he likely thought he'd be living in a house full of screams if he married Maeve. What made her particularly unhappy was that Noah would never know that Violet sang Sunday school songs in a sweet voice and tried to catch birds because she thought they were hungry and she wanted to feed them bread crumbs.

Maeve heard Noah's footsteps as he walked across the room, sounding increasingly distant.

She felt as if her chance for a new life was slipping away.

"It was her father," Maeve blurted out without thinking. She had never meant to tell anyone this part. "He was killed in a brawl at a bar."

Noah turned around, but didn't say anything.

"On the waterfront," she added since he seemed to expect more details. "Violet was sitting in the corner and saw it all."

Noah raised an eyebrow. "Did she follow him there? To the bar?"

Maeve shook her head. This was why she hadn't

wanted to tell him. "My husband was taking care of her and he took her there because he had an—ah—an appointment."

"And the bar owners let her stay?"

"They let people do anything. It wasn't the kind of place most people would go."

"And I remind her of that?"

She shrugged. "I understand many of the men in the brawl had beards. In the dark, that's probably all she saw of their faces."

"She must have been terrified." Noah's voice was tense.

Maeve was silent even though he seemed to be waiting for her to say more. She couldn't confess the rest of it. She didn't want anyone to know the shame of her husband betraying her like he had. It still made her feel ugly.

Finally, Noah walked to the fireplace.

Maeve let the blanket slip down from her head so she could look around. Four large paned windows, two on each outside wall, faced out to the night and she could see the silhouette of trees swaying as the wind blew beside the house.

She hadn't noticed earlier, but now that she searched the shadows, she saw the room was lined with exquisite furniture. Polished Georgian-style settees with rose brocade upholstery and mahogany legs carved in graceful arches. A pair of Louis XVI chairs. Matching side tables with crystal-cut lanterns on them and small silver bowls that she knew were waiting for calling cards and fresh flowers. She'd never expected to find a room like this out here in the territories.

"You must have sent back East for everything." She couldn't gesture because she still held Violet in her arms, but she nodded her head toward the furniture. Lined up straight against the walls, it rivaled what she had seen in the homes that she had cleaned in Boston.

"Steamboat to Fort Benton," Noah said as turned back from his position by the fireplace. "Then mule-drawn wagon to here."

Maeve was so surprised by everything along the walls that her eyes hadn't made their way to the half circle of furniture near where Noah stood.

"You can lie your daughter down here," Noah said with a gesture toward a wooden bench. "If she's quiet enough that she doesn't still need you to hold her."

Maeve blinked, not sure she was seeing things clearly. The more intimate grouping of furniture in front of the fireplace was crudely made. She thought her eyesight was deceiving her until Noah bent over to light a kerosene lantern and the chairs were completely visible.

She had been right. The furniture was what a frontier house would contain—various pieces of unmatched wood, forced together to make a chair or a table, with no thought to beauty or grace. The pieces were not smooth or built to last. Even the lantern looked modest when compared to the crystal globes sitting on the edges of the room.

If it wasn't obvious that the inner circle of chairs was what the man used regularly, Maeve would have been insulted to be led toward such a humble bench in the presence of the outer line of magnificence. She sat down slowly. Violet was heavy in her arms and Maeve hoped she would doze off to sleep.

There would be more time to explore this unusual house in the morning. She wondered if the other parts of the house had this same look of being held back like the occupant was waiting for something to happen before anything was used. She pondered the puzzle of it all for a moment until a realization came to her—of course, the furniture had been for his wife. He'd said she left, but maybe he was hoping she'd come back. Most people, Maeve knew, would sell such fine pieces of furniture if they weren't going to use them.

She looked up to see Noah closing the ivory lace curtains on the room and putting enough wood on the fire to make a small blaze. He then excused himself to go help the men unload the wagon. He gave Violet a sympathetic look before he left the room, but he didn't ask any questions.

The flames from the fire began to slowly warm the air, but Maeve kept the blankets wrapped around her daughter. It had been a tiring day for everyone. More questions had been asked than answered.

She wondered how she and her children were going to be able to live here with a man who had been so in love with his wife that he couldn't marry another woman. In fact, he couldn't even sit on the chairs he'd bought for that woman and likely wouldn't ever sell them since he was hoping she'd come back.

Of course, Maeve thought with a rueful smile to herself, those were only his problems.

She had troubles of her own. A dozen booted men were going back and forth to where she assumed the kitchen was. All of them had beards of some length. A few of them had scars. She expected they all carried knives and some had pistols. Violet might start screaming every time one of these ranch hands crossed her path. The sheer number of men they would be around had not been something Maeve had considered.

She reminded herself that she'd had no other option but to come here. It was this or begging for bread on the streets of Boston. No one ever found enough to survive for long that way. And Violet would likely end up in an orphanage and Maeve in the poorhouse with the baby.

So, she told herself, it was pointless to berate herself for not making a better choice. She'd taken the only path she could.

She bent her head in exhaustion just thinking about the days she had before her, though.

Lord, give me strength, she managed to pray. She could not go further. Her feelings for God had suffered when it had seemed everything had lined up against her in Boston. Some people reported sensing God's care for them in hard times, but all she had felt was an overwhelming silence. It was as if God had been as disappointed in her as her husband must have been to do the things he'd done.

When she'd heard from Noah, she'd begun to think God had decided to be in her life again. And now that future was uncertain.

She had given up any hope of love, but she had believed she would find respect in a new marriage. With God's help, that would be enough for a good life.

She blushed wondering what the ranch hands must think about her now. Noah had said it all very politely, but it was clear that he had called off the wedding, hoping she would grow weary and say she no longer wanted to marry him.

She could only bless the men's hearts for their clear disappointment. They, at least, wanted her to stay. Noah might, too, she assured herself, once he saw how useful she could be.

She heard footsteps and knew Noah was coming back through the hallway. His steps were different from those of the other men. They sounded more confident. Maybe a little quicker. Heavier.

"How long have you had it like this?" Maeve asked when Noah reached the open doorway.

When he didn't answer, she continued, "The wood on these chairs needs to be polished or it will crack and ruin."

"I don't have time to be polishing the furniture."

"I can do it," Maeve offered. After her years working in Boston, there wasn't much she didn't know about caring for expensive furniture. "You want to keep it nice for—"

Her voice trailed off. She wasn't exactly sure she wanted to say the words indicating he was saving the furniture for when his wife returned, but she had no other theory to offer.

Maeve looked down. Her daughter was lying on the bench, with her head in Maeve's lap.

She could feel the man looking at her so she glanced up.

"You must like European furniture," she finished. "It's beautiful."

"Neither," Noah said with a smile. "I bought it to show myself I could."

Maeve wondered how much money the man had.

A dozen men had marched back and forth to the kitchen carrying things past the doorway. Most of the supplies were still coming, but she saw a couple of big bags carried to the back of the house. From the sounds of the steps, two men carried her trunk to the end of the hall. She suspected they had taken it to the bedroom, but the warmth from the fire was making her toes tingle and she didn't want to walk down the hall to see.

She looked around. Back East, she'd rented the smallest room she could find. It had had a bed, two chairs and a stove for heating. She'd barely been able to afford that. This parlor alone was three times the size of her room. She'd brought some of her doilies with her, the ones she'd crocheted for her first wedding. They'd faded over the years and she would be ashamed to even put them out in this house.

She watched as Noah walked out of the room.

He turned and said, "The downstairs bedroom is at the end of the hall. The men are finished unpacking. They'll be leaving in a minute. Don't worry about waking up early. Dakota will be cooking for the men."

Maeve said nothing, but she vowed to be up early enough to make breakfast. She didn't have much time to show Noah how useful she could be and she planned to make the ranch hands the best food they'd ever eaten.

He might not want another wife, she told herself, but he had never wavered on wanting a cook for his men.

The night was black as Noah braced himself against the growing wind and walked as fast as the storm permitted toward the light in the bunkhouse window, thinking about Maeve. She had pursed her lips when he even looked at her inquisitively. She had secrets she still hadn't told him, but he didn't want to press her. He didn't like going to bed with these kinds of mysteries on his mind, though. If he didn't know the problem, he couldn't fix it.

All of the buildings on his ranch were built firm. He'd used milled wood. The planks were measured and cut to fit. That's why there was no dip in the roof of the bunkhouse and there were no gaps in the corners of the side room he'd added to the bunkhouse.

He turned a knob and the door opened. He could see the fire burning in the rock fireplace on the far wall. He stepped inside and stomped the snow off his boots. The group of men sitting by the fire turned in unison to look at him.

He nodded in greeting, wondering how to tell them Reverend Olson might be asking them about him and his sleeping habits.

But the men looked as if they had something on their minds, too.

"Yes?" he asked.

They were silent for a minute and then, Bobby, the youngest ranch hand, let loose.

"We worked hard to get a new cook. And here you are, sending her back. She came for us, too, you know. We wrote the ad."

"Ah," Noah said as he took off his coat and rubbed

the snow off the back of his neck. "But it's me she came to marry."

"Well, she says she's willing," Bobby said in frustration. "The rest is up to you."

Noah walked over to the straight-back chairs gathered around a table and pulled one of them closer to where the men sat. "It doesn't matter whether she's my wife or my cook," Noah said as he settled himself into the chair. "I won't have a woman go back on her agreement with me again. So I want her to be sure she wants to stay here."

The men sat in silence as they considered this.

"You're thinking about that divorce, aren't you?" Dakota finally said from where he sat by the window. "We all know that wasn't your fault. You did everything you could for Allison."

"Did I?" Noah asked them. "Sometimes I wonder. I brought her out here to the ranch and then I left her alone too much. Everyone within a hundred miles of here knew she was unhappy and I didn't take her to town more than once every few months."

"You were busy," Bobby said.

"That's no excuse." Noah gave him a smile. "Someday, when you're married, you'll understand. Marriage is a commitment that isn't always easy."

"Have you been talking to Mrs. Barker?" Dakota asked as he walked over to Noah and peered at him as if he was trying to determine the state of his soul.

Noah squirmed. The older woman was the biggest gossip in the area. "She was at the church this morning, but that's all. Why?"

The men looked at Dakota and he looked back at them.

Finally, the other man shrugged. "She told me her husband saw your Allison down in Denver last week when he was there on railroad business. She goes by Alice now, but it was her all right. Mr. Barker told her you were getting yourself a new bride. Mrs. Barker said it didn't sound like Allison—or Alice, I guess—was too happy about that."

"I'm sure she was only making some polite response. You know how Mrs. Barker likes to add to the truth to make the telling of something more dramatic."

"I don't know," Dakota muttered. "I can still hear Allison complaining. The table was too rough. The sun was too hot. No one came to visit. The cows had flies. The flowers didn't grow."

"She hoped for more out of life than me," Noah said ruefully. "She knew how much land I owned and she pictured herself entertaining governors and other important people. The only one who ever came out to see us was Mrs. Barker and I am grateful to her for that."

"Ranch women know what to expect," Dakota said firmly.

Noah nodded. "That's just it. Maeve lived in Boston for most of her life, except for a few years in

Ireland when she was young. She hasn't even had a chance to think of what life here would be like."

It was quiet again as the men considered that.

"I'd sure hate to lose her," Bobby said.

"We don't even know for sure that she can cook," another ranch hand said philosophically.

"With hair like that, I'm not worried," a different cowboy said. "Irish women are born cooking."

"I know she can do better than Dakota," Bobby said with a look at Dakota.

"I'd like to see you make a flapjack worth eating," the older ranch hand retorted with no rancor in his voice.

Noah knew a lot of bickering went on in the bunkhouse and he usually turned a deaf ear to it. He'd had a long day himself and was looking forward to slipping into bed and sleeping.

"The Reverend Olson might be talking to some of you." Noah didn't have to look around to know he'd caught their full attention. The reverend was respected around here. "He says you're to be my chaperones. Make sure I sleep in the room off the bunkhouse and don't go to the house at night."

Bobby grinned. "So the preacher is worried you might want to be more married than you think."

Noah felt the tension shoot through his jaw. "He's not meaning me particularly. He just knows the value of a woman's reputation in these parts. For that matter, I should make sure none of you leave the bunkhouse for long periods of time at night, either."

"You can count on us," the men chorused in unison. "We'll take care of her."

Noah looked at them skeptically.

"Do you think she should be cooking for us tomorrow at all?" Bobby asked then, his hand going up to scratch his head. "She looked pretty tired."

"As far as I'm concerned, you can treat her like a lady of leisure tomorrow," Noah said. "She doesn't need to cook. Show her we're friendly around here. Fix her up a cup of tea in the afternoon."

The men nodded their heads and Noah reached up to feel his beard.

"Whoever gets up first, fill the washbasin with water and set it on the stove to heat," he said. "We're all shaving our beards off tomorrow morning before we leave the bunkhouse."

"What?" the men protested in near unison.

"You want us to freeze our faces?" Dakota demanded to know. "It'll be a hard winter if I read the signs right."

"The little girl is afraid of men with beards," Noah said. "That's why she screamed."

The men were silent for a moment.

"That was the worst scream I ever heard," Bobby finally said. "I've heard trapped animals show less terror. I guess I can give up my whiskers."

The other men nodded.

"Thank you," Noah said with no small satisfaction. He'd done what he could to help his guests. Tomorrow was another day.

He walked over to the door that led to the private room and went inside, closing the door behind him. Even though he was tired, he couldn't resist looking out the window facing the house. He saw a faint light in his bedroom. Maeve must have the lantern with her as she went to bed. If Maeve was going to learn that ranch life wasn't for her, it would be good if she did it soon. It would sure ease his mind to have his hopes cut down before they started to grow inside him.

Chapter Four

Hours later, Maeve lay in bed, the darkness all around her, and gave thanks for the warmth of the blankets. Her daughter was curled up beside her and she could no longer hear the wind blowing outside. Dim light, the kind that came just before dawn, was starting to shine through the frost-covered windows. She was going to get up in a few minutes. She planned to show the men what a good cook she was and she knew they ate early. Sliding away from Violet gently so she wouldn't wake the child, she reached for a spare quilt that was sitting on the chair by the bed.

She pulled the quilt to her and then sat up, wrapping it around her. She'd never known the luxury of having a spare blanket and she marveled at the bounty found in this house. The bedroom had none of the discord of the parlor. All of the furniture here, from the bed with its peeled log frame to the wide dresser made of walnut, had been built by a craftsman, but it wasn't made for show. There were no carved vines to gather dust and no inlaid marble. She doubted the desires of his wife had influenced Noah to buy any of the furniture in this room.

Last night, she had explored the kitchen and realized that cooking for the ranch hands took place in the main house. A solid plank table, the boards pressed together so they met perfectly, stood in a large room off the work area. At least twenty people could sit up to the table with the benches and chairs arranged around it. At the end of the room, a shelf held stacks of heavy white plates and bowls—the kind of dishes the servants used back East. In the center of the table, a jar of honey and several sets of salt and pepper shakers were grouped together.

Maeve stood and bent over to light the lantern on the stand by the bed. She kept the flame turned down so she wouldn't waken Violet. She did not need much light anyway.

She walked over to the side wall and opened the lid of her trunk before slipping her hands down to where she kept her two work dresses. They were black cotton dresses with full white aprons, freshly washed, starched and ironed each week. The lady of the house where Maeve had done most of her heavy work insisted that all the women on her staff wear black dresses with white aprons. Not that she paid for the clothing, of course. Fortunately, the cook had outgrown a couple of dresses and offered them to Maeve. She was grateful even though they had been washed so often the dye was faded in spots and the cuffs on the sleeves were frayed.

The lady had given Maeve a critical look when she first saw her in one of the dresses. The woman didn't refuse to let her wear them, although she had added the requirement of a white cap to cover Maeve's copper-colored hair. Her employer would have bleached the freckles from Maeve's face and the pink from her cheeks if she'd been able. A servant, the woman had said that same day with her lips pressed together in disapproval, shouldn't look too colorful since a proper maid blended into the background so her betters would be the ones to gather the admiring glances.

Maeve pulled a dress and an apron out of the trunk and set them on the chair by the bed. She wasn't going to wear a cap. She would pull her hair back and put a net around the bun she made, but she wasn't going to be a servant in this house. Or anywhere else likely. After she'd lost her job, no other house in Boston would even talk to her when she called at the servant's door to ask for employment. The newspapers had ensured that the whole city was aware of the shame her husband had brought to their name.

That was all in the past, though, Maeve told

herself as she washed, fixed her hair securely and dressed. She had hung her gray dress up last night and she checked it to be sure it was drying. While she was thinking of it, she took the sprig of mistletoe out of the dress pocket and set it on the low dresser. Even if it didn't result in any kissing, the sprig would be a fond Christmas decoration for her.

Violet turned over a few times, but she stayed sleeping as her mother quietly moved around the room doing a few other things. Maeve had heard the back door to the house open a few minutes ago and now a board creaked as someone walked on the kitchen floor.

She went over and kissed Violet on the forehead.

"Mommy's going to be close by," she whispered, thinking how she'd dreamed of being able to say those words to her daughter as she headed off to work. She could be a proper mother for the first time in years, able to hear any call Violet might give.

Maeve left the lantern burning low when she exited the room. The kitchen was only a few feet down the side hall from the bedroom and she'd heard more sounds. She'd put on her leather shoes because they were still damp and she didn't want them to shrink as they dried. The heels clicked on the plank floor so she knew Dakota, who was likely the one who was in the kitchen, would be expecting her.

The door to the kitchen was closed so she gave a soft knock. She didn't want to startle the older man.

She didn't wait for an answer before she pushed the door open.

"Oh."

It wasn't Dakota.

The blaze in the cast-iron cookstove gave off some light because the firebox in the front of the stove was wide-open. Maeve had to step closer before she could truly see, though.

"Noah?" she asked.

The man stood there with his shirt unbuttoned and a towel draped over his shoulder. His hair was tousled and his beard was covered with what looked like white soap. He stood by the stove with a kettle in one hand and a bucket in the other.

"I'm boiling water," he whispered. "I didn't want to wake you up. You should be in bed asleep."

"I got up to make breakfast." She squared her shoulders so she'd look ready to work and took a step toward him. "I plan to make coffee so I can do that for you."

Noah shook his head. "The water's for washing up."

Maeve looked down at the top of the stove then and noticed that several pans and kettles were boiling. Steam was rising up from them into the cold air of the kitchen.

Noah moved a kettle on the stove and uncovered the open circle where a burner usually was. A golden light flared as a piece of wood snapped and she could see Noah clearly in the surrounding darkness. His eyes were watching her and there was a kindness in them that she hadn't seen before. Maybe he was getting used to her, she thought hopefully.

"I wanted to have this all done before you got up," he explained.

"I can help," Maeve offered as she reached for handle of one of the pans.

"You have a child to take care of," Noah said as he took the handle from her. "That's work enough for anyone."

Maeve hesitated. "Violet will be fine. She just needs a little time to get used to where she is."

Taking a deep breath, Maeve continued, "Sometimes I think it might help to have another child around. Someone for Violet to play with."

Noah shrugged. "I didn't have any brothers or sisters and I did fine."

"So you don't like lots of children?" Maeve whispered, her heart sinking.

Noah didn't answer because the back door leading to the kitchen opened again and a dark shape came into the room.

"That'll be Dakota," Noah said to her and then turned to the ranch hand. "What do you think? Does Violet need another child around to play with?"

The cowboy stood still in the darkened doorway.

"I know more about calves and any kind of animal than I do a little girl," Dakota finally spoke.

"But most young'uns like to have another young'un to race around the corral with."

Noah shook his head. "I can't see Violet racing around the barn so I think she's fine being just one child."

Maeve wished she'd never asked.

"I can handle breakfast by myself," Maeve told the older man. She wanted to show Noah she could do the job. Her friend, the cook in the house in Boston, had shown her how to make some elegant dishes just in case Maeve ever landed a better position in another house. If they had the ingredients, she could make eggs Benedict, a recipe from Delmonico's Restaurant in New York City.

"He's not here to cook breakfast," Noah said as he gestured for the ranch hand to come closer to them. "He's taking water back to the bunkhouse. They can't boil it fast enough over there."

Maeve adjusted her assumptions about how clean the cowboys were. Maybe they were taking baths.

"Isn't it awfully cold?" she asked.

"The blizzard ran itself out in the middle of the night," Dakota said as he walked up to where Maeve and Noah were standing. "I think today is going to be nice enough. Might even get the supplies delivered if the mercantile can spare Jimmy."

Dakota's face was easy to see, too, when he was close enough to the fire. The years had taken their toll on him. She wondered if Noah had assigned him to be the cook to give him some relief from the harder work outside. He was spry enough, though. The cowboy wore suspenders as he stood there. They were loose and hung down to his sides instead of being tight upon his shoulders. She noticed he had a bar of soap in one hand.

Just then Maeve heard Violet calling her.

"Mommy," the girl repeated herself with more volume. She sounded afraid.

"I have to go," Maeve said as she started toward the door. "She was asleep last night when I put her to bed and she'll wonder where she is."

"Might as well get some more sleep yourself," Noah called after her. "Breakfast will be late this morning."

Maeve stepped into the bedroom and rushed to her daughter.

"It's all right," she assured the child as she bent down to hug her. "We're safe here. And I've got you."

Maeve took off her dress and apron, draping them over the nearby chair. Then she lay down on the bed and cuddled Violet close to her. She could feel the beat of the girl's heart slow as she relaxed. Noah was right. It wouldn't hurt to lie here for a few more minutes. The sight of him standing there by the stove had her flustered anyway. It was likely the darkness that added the feeling of intimacy, but it was disconcerting anyway.

She listened to the sounds of Noah and Dakota

talking as she watched Violet fall back to sleep. Maeve couldn't hear what the two men were saying, but the sound of their voices quickly lulled her to sleep, as well.

Meanwhile, Noah almost burned his fingers on the handle of the latest kettle. He drew his hand back with a soft hiss and shook it before reaching for a kitchen towel.

"It's going to blister," he said to Dakota, who was pouring water from the bucket into another pan.

Noah held out the towel to the ranch hand. "Put some cold on this."

"You got to pay attention when you deal with hot water," the cowboy said as he did as asked.

Noah took the wet towel and wrapped it around his finger to stop the throbbing.

"Got to pay attention about other things, too," Dakota added.

Noah looked up at him. "What other things?"

The ranch hand jerked his head toward the hallway that led to the main bedroom. "Reverend Olson is going to be asking us if you're keeping to your word and staying in the bunkhouse."

"I don't think the reverend meant I couldn't come into my own kitchen to boil some water," Noah protested. "Besides, I thought she would still be asleep. It's chilly being up this early in the morning and I know she had a hard day yesterday." Noah realized he was talking too much, but he couldn't seem to stop. "I had no reason to think she'd be anywhere but asleep."

Dakota shrugged. "All I'm saying is that a man can start out innocent enough and land into trouble."

"Not me," Noah said emphatically. "I know better than to lose my head."

This time the ranch hand turned to look at him. "Is that right?"

The question hung in the air, but Noah didn't argue any further. All he said was, "Allison is long gone from here."

"I wasn't talking about Allison," Dakota said as he set the empty bucket back on the cupboard by the door.

Noah figured as much. He wasn't sure what he felt about Maeve, but his men probably saw the confusion on his face.

"We're running a ranch here," Noah finally said. "We have enough to worry about."

Dakota grunted, but he didn't say anything more as he picked up a boiling kettle of water and walked toward the door.

Just before the other man left the kitchen, he said, "If all we were worrying about was the cattle, we wouldn't be scraping our faces this morning. They don't care about our beards."

With that, the ranch hand stepped outside.

Noah was left alone in the kitchen. He hadn't paid

any attention to this room for months and now he saw that it had grown a little shabby. Dakota had used the towels to grab too many skillets off the stove when the eggs or biscuits were burning. Scorch marks stained every one of the five towels he could see. By his recollection, another three had burst into flames at one time or the other.

He'd taken the curtains off the windows last winter when some of the hems had come out and they'd started to sag. As he recalled, Allison had liked to keep jars filled with wildflowers on the table. Those jars now held bullet casings on the bottom shelf in the supply room. The ranch hands almost always milked two or three cows, but no one had bothered to make butter in a long time and there was dust on the churn that sat in the corner by the broom.

He walked over to that corner and decided the broom needed replacing, as well.

He felt the lather stiffening in his beard, but he sat down anyway. He did not know when he had let his house fall into disarray. He had been upset when Allison left him, and his pride had stung even worse when she'd divorced him. But long before that he had known she had married him with false impressions in her mind. Little of her heart had made her decision to marry him or leave him. He was a plan that hadn't worked out for her.

On his part, he had been ignorant, he supposed. Allison was the most beautiful woman he'd ever seen and it had seemed wrong to question his good fortune when she'd hinted she would marry him if he asked. Like he had told Dakota and Maeve, he had been an only child. His parents had both died in a carriage accident when he was eight years old. He had been passed back and forth between two elderly great aunts until he had been judged old enough to make his own way at sixteen.

Neither of the aunts had spoken with him much. Fortunately, they'd each had a gardener who had taken him under their wings. From the one, he'd learned about growing plants. From the other, he'd learned how to take care of goats and then the milk cows.

He had not known what a family felt like, though, so he had been glad to marry Allison.

Now he wondered if he hadn't missed too much growing up to ever be a good husband or father. Allison had certainly found him lacking. His ranch hands had taught him something about loyalty and the contentment that comes from caring about others, but there was more to family than that. He knew Mrs. Barker had advised him once to share what was in his heart—his fears and dreams—with Allison in hopes of improving their marriage. That hadn't worked well, though.

Chapter Five

Maeve stretched her legs while her eyes were still closed. The bed was warm and Violet was still sleeping. There were no sounds from the kitchen so Maeve guessed Dakota had not started breakfast for the men yet—which was the way she wanted it to be.

When she opened her eyes, she saw that the sun had risen.

She rolled over to the edge of the bed and sat up.

This was the first time she'd seen the bedroom in full light and she was delighted with the golden hue of the logs that made up the outside walls. A bearskin hung near the doorway to the hall. A dozen books were sitting on a shelf next to the bed. One of them was a Bible. Another the works of Charles Dickens.

Maeve reached over and pulled her dress and apron to her so she could put them on again. Within a few minutes, she had her shoes on, too, and was ready to go to the kitchen. She wanted to be there before Dakota came so she could find out where the supplies were kept.

Sunlight was streaming into the kitchen when she walked through the door. The air was steamy, but there were no more kettles boiling on the stove. The fire was going though so it would be easy to fry up some bacon before she started on the eggs.

She went into the side room that served as a pantry. There was a large bag of flour and a smaller one of sugar. A jar of honey, like the one on the table, stood in the corner of a shelf. What looked like twenty tins of oysters and a big jar of pickles were next to it. Empty bags were lying on the other shelves.

Deciding that there must be another place for food that needed to be kept cold, Maeve pushed against the door that led to the outside. As she suspected, there was a small room with yet another door that gave final exit to the outdoors. Between the two doors was a little room where a cabinet hugged one wall and a bench the other. A tall shelf over the bench had an assortment of hats on it.

When she opened the cabinet door she saw it was lined with tin. She could feel the air inside was cooler than in the kitchen. Vents were cut to let in the outside air. A side of bacon sat on one shelf, a ham was hanging from a hook in an open area and several large jars of milk, a thick layer of cream on top each, were on another shelf with pieces of cheesecloth draped over them. A washbasin filled with a mound of eggs, both brown and white, was by the milk. She figured there were easily four dozen eggs and five gallons of milk.

On the train, Mercy had assured her that a rancher like Noah would have an abundance of food and she was right. Maeve reached up carefully and started putting eggs in the pocket of her apron. She couldn't wait to give Violet a cup of that milk. Her daughter hadn't tasted any since Maeve lost her job. Instead, they had made do with watery bean soup and the foodstuffs her friend had given them.

Before long, Maeve had found a sharp knife and sliced up enough bacon to fill three cast-iron skillets. She put the pans on the cookstove and was lining up thirty eggs to crack when she felt the first tremble of unease in her stomach. She told herself it was nothing.

The bacon started to sizzle so she opened a drawer looking for a fork to turn the meat when it was browned on one side. She figured if she ignored her queasiness, it would go away.

While the bacon fried, she went in search of a pot to make coffee. She found two of them on a high shelf in the pantry. They looked clean, but she took them to the basin to wash anyway. A small bag of coffee was in the cupboard by the basin.

Before long, the smell of the bacon mixed with

that of the coffee. She walked over to the stove and used a long fork to put the cooked bacon slices on a platter. She slipped that plate into the small warming oven on top of the stove. She poured most of the bacon grease out of the skillets before cracking eggs and dropping them into the hot pans.

She had managed to ignore the nausea that plagued her until she had all the eggs cooking. Then, looking down at the thirty yolks, a wave of it rolled over her and made her clutch her stomach. She knew she had to sit down.

Just then, the back door swung open and Dakota stepped inside.

She had her eyes on the closest chair in the side area where the table was and she began walking over there. She couldn't even think about greeting the ranch hand until she sat down and took a deep breath. She'd be fine if she just closed her eyes for a few minutes.

She barely had herself settled on the chair when she saw Dakota looming over her.

"What's wrong?" he asked as he leaned down.

"Nothing," she managed to whisper and then wondered if something was wrong with her eyes.

The ranch hand had lost his beard. At least she thought he'd had one. Maybe in the dark last night she'd been confused. But it had seemed as if all the men wore beards, some scruffy and some trimmed, but all distinctly there. And then she saw the nicks on his face like the ones her husband used to get when he went to the barber around the corner who didn't have much experience.

"You shaved!" she said.

Dakota didn't even respond. He was looking at her as if he was trying to figure something out. He was frowning for a full minute, examining her, when his face cleared and he smiled.

"You're pregnant," he said with a grin.

His pronouncement was enough to make Maeve sit up straighter in the chair. "How'd you know?"

"I was married once, a long time ago. I'd know that color of green on your face anywhere."

"You can't tell anyone!"

"We're going to have a baby!" Dakota kept grinning. "Right here on the ranch."

Then his face fell. "Noah doesn't know, does he?"

She shook her head. "I don't think he even wants a baby. You heard him this morning. He was an only child and he thinks that's fine."

"Oh, I wouldn't take his words to heart," Dakota said as he reached up to rub the beard that wasn't there and then put his hand back down. "Noah is a good man. He'll do what's right."

Maeve just shook her head. It was hard to imagine anything drearier than someone doing his duty for her, especially when Noah didn't owe her any duty. She wasn't quite sure how these mail-order-bride agreements worked, but she understood from others that no one was obligated to go through with the wedding.

"You can't tell him," she repeated.

Just then Maeve smelled something burning.

"The eggs!" she exclaimed as she started to stand.

"You just sit there," Dakota said as he straightened up. "I'll get them."

"No, I need to make breakfast," she told the ranch hand, feeling panicked. "Noah needs a cook. I want him to see that I'm useful."

"You're in no condition to—" Dakota started and then stopped to listen.

Maeve heard the back door to the kitchen open then and the sound of boots as the men stomped the snow off of them. She took a deep breath and forced herself to stand. She walked over to the stove while the men were still in the entry room.

Dakota slipped something into her hands as they started coming into the kitchen. No one saw him.

Maeve smiled and waved the spoon he'd given her around. If anyone was thinking, they would realize that no one used a spoon to fry eggs, but she was counting on the men all being sleepy still. It was seldom anyone thought about the cook, and especially what utensils she used to make the food.

By now, Dakota had turned over all of the eggs. The edges were burned black and the middles a hard yellow. Maeve wasn't sure anyone could eat them.

The men shuffled their feet as they stood in the

middle of the floor. The last man to come into the kitchen was Noah. Seeing his face without his beard suddenly made her realize.

"You shaved your beards," she exclaimed, her gaze going from man to man. "Every one of you."

They all suddenly took an interest in the floor and looked sheepish. Or maybe it was that they seemed younger with their skin so white where their whiskers had been and so dark on the rest of their faces.

"We can get by without them," Bobby finally said. "They're only whiskers."

Maeve turned to Noah. She knew he had been the one to ask the men to shave off their facial hair to make it easier for Violet.

"Thank you," she whispered as she took a step toward him, blinking a little so no one would see her eyes were damp.

Noah nodded back, but didn't say anything.

They looked at each other and Maeve thought she might break down and really cry. No man had ever done something so kind for her. And his eyes were steady, as though he understood.

Finally, when it seemed they would go on gazing at each other forever, Noah took a step toward her and bent down slightly to give her a kiss on her cheek.

Maeve put her hand up to the place his lips had touched. She knew it couldn't be, but it felt warmer there than the rest of her face.

By then the ranch hands had moved through the kitchen and she heard them sitting down at the table. Almost at the same time, Bobby was taking the plates from the shelf and passing them down the line until everyone had one. Then he did the same thing with a jar that held the forks and another that held knives.

So far the ranch hands had not noticed that she and Noah were standing together. Maeve stepped back a little, certain they had not seen the kiss. She liked that it had been private, something just between her and Noah.

"We'll probably want spoons, too," Maeve suggested as she took another step toward the table. She wished she had more to offer the men for breakfast.

She looked back at Noah and he smiled at her. Then she turned to the young man in front of her. "The spoons are right here."

"Yes, ma'am," Bobby said shyly.

In a few minutes, most of the men were sitting down in their chairs. They had left two places empty in the corner closest to the kitchen and another across the table from them.

"This one's for you, Dakota," one of the men pointed to the lone seat.

That left Noah and Maeve standing.

Smiling even wider, Noah walked over and pulled out one of the remaining chairs for her.

Maeve nodded her thanks as she sat in it. Maybe the men had seen the kiss, after all.

Noah sat down and moved his chair closer to her so that their elbows touched.

Dakota carried in the two platters and set them on the table. The eggs and bacon looked forlorn, Maeve thought as she saw them.

"Thanks to whoever prepared this," Noah said without looking at the food.

Maeve glanced at Dakota and then back at the burnt edges of the eggs. She knew the ranch hand was planning to take the blame for the meal, but she glanced at him and shook her head slightly.

"I'm the one who ruined the meal," Maeve said.

The men looked up in unison at that announcement. It didn't take long for dismay to fill their faces. They looked as if they had lost their last chance at good cooking, she thought.

"Let's all pray," Noah said quietly.

Maeve was used to holding hands when she prayed, usually just with Violet, but she stilled the impulse as everyone bowed their heads.

"Father, we thank You for Your goodness to us," Noah said, his voice sincere. "Help us to live in ways that please You. We thank You for Your provisions for us. Bless this food. In Jesus's name, Amen."

The men murmured in agreement as they looked up and opened their eyes.

"At least she didn't burn any biscuits," Maeve heard one of the men mutter mournfully to another. "They're my last hope."

She smiled. "Maybe tomorrow."

The men grinned with her.

"All I know is that you better appreciate these eggs," Dakota said as he started to pass the platters around. "These will be the last eggs we eat for a while."

"Huh?" Half of the men responded in shock. The others just sat there with their mouths open.

"We're going to take all the eggs and get some hens to sitting on them," Dakota declared. "We need some babies around here."

The smile on Maeve's face froze. She cast a frantic look toward Dakota.

"Baby chicks?" Bobby asked the older ranch hand in further astonishment.

Dakota nodded. "We need babies of any kind."

Maeve listened carefully, but Noah didn't say another word.

"I need to go see to Violet," Maeve said as she nodded politely to all of the men.

She stood and walked with dignity until she got through the bedroom door. Then she fought her queasiness and her tears. She dampened a cloth in the washbasin and put it on her forehead. She didn't want Noah to see her like this. She hoped God was looking, though. She could use His help.

* * *

Noah knew leadership wasn't always easy, but his men relied on him so he slid two eggs off the platter and started to eat them. He finally decided they were the worst eggs he'd ever eaten. The crispy black on the down side of the fried eggs made it impossible to taste the regular part. Not that the regular part looked all that appealing, either.

"They're very good," Noah said, hoping no one questioned him. "Adequate anyway."

The men didn't say anything.

"Going without eggs for a while, might be good," he added as he unsuccessfully tried to cut the egg with his fork.

"I knew you'd see it my way," Dakota said with jubilation in his voice. "You'll like seeing all the babies around here. Maybe we can get some kittens, too. All kinds of babies."

Noah looked at the ranch hand. Something more was going on here than Dakota was saying, but the other man wasn't saying what it was.

"You missing your boy?" Noah asked. The cowboy's son, who was almost thirty, was working in Chicago as a butcher. Dakota was very proud of him and his grandsons.

"You can never have too many children," the ranch hand said.

Which wasn't really an answer, Noah realized, so he was silent for a moment.

"But what are we going to eat for breakfast?" Bobby asked in dismay, clearly impatient with all the talk of children and baby chickens.

No one else was even attempting to eat their eggs. A few had picked up a slice of bacon. Even though that was charred, the bacon broke off into manageable pieces.

"Christmas gruel," Dakota answered emphatically as he put a bit of bacon in his mouth. "It's served at Christmas in that story by Charles Dickens. The one with all the orphan children. Having such a hard time. It's in the book Noah has. Gruel is good for the holidays."

"They only ate that because they had nothing else to eat," Bobby protested.

Dakota nodded. "Like us."

"I don't even know what's in it," Bobby lamented.

"Oats and water," Dakota assured him. "Maybe some wheat if we can find any in the barn."

So far, all the men except Bobby were treating Dakota's suggestion as a joke. The more time that went by, though, he could see their uncertainty rise.

Noah knew he was going to have to do something or he would have a full-blown mutiny on his hands. Besides, it was cold outside today and would be tomorrow. His men needed to check on the cattle in the ravine north of here. He had some crackers and beef jerky they could take for their noon meal, but they couldn't go without breakfast for many days.

"The coffee is good," he told the men. "And I'll talk to Maeve about making us some pancakes tomorrow."

"Pancakes are easy," Bobby said in relief. "She can make them without any problems."

"That woman shouldn't be cooking," Dakota declared emphatically.

"Why's that?" Noah looked at his ranch hand, but the man didn't say anything more. "If anyone has anything against Mrs. Flanagan, they should say so now."

"What?" several of them asked in shock.

"Of course we don't," the others said.

All of the men looked at him with accusation in their eyes, likely wondering if he had something against her.

"I'm not suggesting you needed to have anything to say," he told them. "She seems like a perfectly fine woman."

Dakota snorted. "She's better than that. And if you're not going to court her properly, I intend to find someone who will."

Noah felt his breath leave him. His men knew too much. "I didn't mean to give the impression I'm not going to court her."

"Well, that's what she thinks," Dakota said, not giving an inch in his stance.

"I'll talk to her, then, and make sure she knows the decision is hers," Noah finally said.

That seemed to make the men relax.

"Bobby," Noah said as he turned to the ranch hand. "There are some cans of peaches in the front closet. I was saving them for Christmas, but I think we're close enough. Go ahead and bring a can for each of us."

"It would be my pleasure," the younger man said as he stood up quickly and began to walk.

Everyone looked happier at that news.

The men took their knives out and opened their cans of peaches. After they ate them, they each took some strips of beef jerky and crackers wrapped in a clean bandanna pouch for their noon meal, and left the kitchen. None of them said much, although Dakota did give him a strange look. All of them would be saddled and looking over the cattle soon enough. Ordinarily, Noah would ride with them, but today he wanted to stay home with Maeve and Violet and make sure they had everything they needed to be comfortable.

He hadn't opened his can of peaches, so he dug in his pocket for his knife and started jabbed the point of it into the tin lid of the can.

Then he heard a shuffling noise behind him. The sun was shining into the room in full force now and the smell of burnt bacon had not gone away.

He turned around and Violet stood there in a white nightgown with a long ruffle at the bottom of it. Her eyes were solemn and he could tell she was ready to turn and run at the slightest hint of trouble.

"My mommy says knives aren't nice," the girl said, her voice reproachful.

"They can be bad," Noah agreed as he put his down on the table. "But I'm using this one to open a can of peaches. Do you like peaches?"

Violet's gaze did not waver. "My daddy was killed with a knife."

Noah turned his chair so he was facing the child. "I know. And I'm sorry you had to see that."

The girl did not say anything, but he could see her studying him.

"Your face isn't scary anymore," she finally said.

"I shaved," he agreed. "And so did all of the other men who live here."

She nodded and took a step toward him.

"My mommy cried when my daddy died," she informed him, standing much closer to him.

"I'm sure she did."

Noah was glad that Dakota had left the fire going in the cookstove. The girl was barefoot and, while her nightgown had long sleeves, she had to be chilly. If he didn't think he'd frighten her, he'd offer to give her his vest for extra warmth.

Just then he heard another cry and looked up to see Maeve rushing down the hall toward her daughter. She ran to Violet and knelt down beside her daughter.

Then she turned to Noah.

"I'm so sorry," she said, frantically. "I hope she didn't bother you."

"Of course not." Noah was almost offended. He would have gone on to explain that he wanted her and Violet here, but Maeve had already put her arm around the girl and was shepherding her back to the bedroom.

Within minutes, Maeve came back out in the hallway. She was trying to smooth back the copper curls flying around her head and straighten the white apron that had gotten twisted around her waist.

Noah smiled. He hadn't seen such an enchanting scene in his whole life.

By the time she stood in front of him, though, she was all tidied up. Her hair was forced into some kind of a net. Her apron was right where it belonged. And all of the charm had gone out of her. She was stiff and formal.

"I'm so sorry," she repeated the words she'd said earlier. "I fell asleep and Violet got away. It won't happen again."

Noah's heart sank. She was acting as if she was a servant in his home. That wasn't what he'd intended, even though he knew the ad made it sound that way.

"You are my guests," he said. "I want you to feel like this is your home. Violet is free to wander about."

Maeve nodded, but she looked at him uncertainly.

Noah suddenly realized that she would never relax as long as he was in the house. He stood up and was careful to take his knife off the table and fold the blade down so he could put it into his pocket.

"I have some work to do in the barn," he said. "If you need anything just step outside and holler. The men took food with them and won't be back until supper."

She nodded and he saw the relief in her eyes.

He turned and walked away then. He had some bridles he could mend and it wouldn't hurt to clean out the milk stalls. He had to admit, though, that he'd rather spend the day in the house with Maeve and Violet. Maybe he'd have been able to sneak another kiss.

Chapter Six

Maeve was determined to show Noah that she knew how to cook. She'd gone back to the kitchen after he left and sat at the table, letting her gaze wander around the large room. Even some of the houses in Boston didn't have a kitchen this big. A dinner there usually included fish and beef. Maybe potatoes and a root vegetable. Fresh berries if it was summer. Or a pudding for dessert if it was winter.

She'd never eaten those meals, but the cook had described them to her in great detail. Not that she'd be able to make food like that here. She didn't have the supplies.

But she'd seen a bag of flour and she had some sourdough starter tucked away in a jar in the corner of her trunk. Once she got the skillets and platters washed, she would make bread. She didn't think anyone had baked anything in this house for a long time. She suspected everything had been fried.

She stood up and looked around the table again. Not many of the dishes had been used. She'd just stack the clean plates and put the utensils back in the jars.

She figured a ranch like this would have a root cellar, too, and she'd noticed a mound of earth to the east of the house that was likely it. She'd explore that and see what they had.

By the time the sun was high in the sky, Maeve had finished. Ten round loaves of sourdough bread were cooling on the table. She'd churned enough cream to make four large mounds of butter. The root cellar had potatoes, carrots and onions so she'd made two big pans of stew. She normally would have used some beef or rabbit with it, but she had neither. Instead, she cut bacon into small pieces and added that for flavor.

Once the cooking was done, Maeve found a mop and washed the plank flooring in the kitchen and the hall. Then she scrubbed the wood table where everyone ate.

Violet came out and decided to play doll with a long pillow she'd found in the parlor. She put Maeve's black hat on the top of it and tied a red bandanna around its middle for a dress. She then got the mistletoe off the dresser and practiced giving her doll a Christmas kiss under it. Maeve just shook her head and laughed.

Finally, the girl went to take a nap and Maeve finished her work.

By that time, perspiration was dripping off her face. The fabric of her black dress stuck to her. She had her hair tied back and she had smudges on her white apron where she'd wiped her hands after rinsing out the mop.

When she heard the rap on the front door, she almost bolted to the bedroom. But then the person knocked again. She figured it was someone to see Noah and he hadn't heard them come up to the house. Then she realized it might be someone who needed help. The storm had passed, but there was a lot of snow on the ground.

At the third knock, Maeve went to the door and opened it.

"Oh," she breathed out in wonder.

The most beautiful woman she'd ever seen was standing there. Her jet-black hair was twisted into a perfect knot and a dove-colored hat swooped down over her delicate face. The brim of the hat was decorated with bright red ribbon. Her overcoat of pearl gray matched a silk dress of the same color underneath. The silk shimmered with every slight movement the woman made, and she was adjusting the coat on her shoulders so the silk was a constant change of color.

Maeve was speechless—which didn't matter as the woman clearly intended to speak.

"I understand this is Noah Miller's house," she said, not even waiting for Maeve to nod before adding, "Tell him that his wife is here."

"Oh," Maeve repeated. This was the woman who had left Noah. And now she was back. Maeve was poised to make some remark about the sanctity of marriage when the woman spoke again.

"I see Noah finally decided I was right and that he needed some domestic help." The woman paused to eye Maeve's dress and apron with disapproval. "I assume you have some references so, if you work out, I will keep you on. I can't imagine where else we would find a maid out here in this wilderness."

Maeve could feel the pink rise on her cheeks. The woman had so much incorrect that Maeve almost didn't know where to start.

"This is not a wilderness," Maeve began her protest. "And, no, I don't have references. But I don't need them because—"

Just then, Maeve heard two sets of boots stomping through the house. She turned and there was Noah and Jimmy, the boy from the mercantile, charging down the hallway until they both stood behind her in the doorway.

"What are you doing here?" Noah demanded from her left side.

"I thought you might need some help celebrating Christmas," the woman said with a flirtatious smile. "You never bothered to do anything special for

Christmas when we were married," Noah said and Maeve could tell he'd crossed his arms because she felt one of them touch her back. "Why would you do anything now?"

"I've been lonely for you," she said, summoning up a tear.

Maeve didn't want to watch any more of the performance. She supposed she should be happy. Noah had his wife back and he could finally start living in his parlor. He'd clearly been waiting for the woman. But Maeve knew one thing for sure. She wasn't going to work in this house for that woman.

Turning so she could leave, Maeve stepped back so that Noah and Jimmy were suddenly in front of her.

"I'm just here with the delivery," Jimmy said then, obviously nervous to be that close to the conflict. He looked at Noah. "She called herself Alice Miller. She said she's your wife. I knew she couldn't be, but she insisted I give her a ride out here and I didn't know what to do—"

So her name was Alice, was it? Maeve thought sourly. She'd always liked the name Alice until now.

Noah wasn't paying any attention to Jimmy's stuttered excuses. Instead, he was staring at the woman.

"He left you, didn't he?" Noah demanded to know. "That man you said was a judge. The one you divorced me to marry? What was his name?"

Alice shrugged. "Judge Brandon Scott of Denver.

No, he didn't leave me. I'm the one who left him. I should have known he wouldn't measure up to you. He didn't even—" She leaned closer to Noah. "You know I've always liked a man who has assets."

Noah looked at the woman with enough disgust to warm Maeve's heart. She decided she would stay for a few minutes, after all.

"Don't tell me you left him because he's broke," Noah said. "And I suppose you married him, too."

Alice looked startled at that. "Of course I married him. I'd have no standing at all when he died if I didn't. No one thought he'd lose his job."

Noah shook his head.

"Don't worry, though," the woman assured him. "It's not that hard to get a divorce. We did."

"You're going back on the wagon with Jimmy," Noah said decisively.

"But I'm hungry," Alice protested, clearly surprised that she'd been ordered to leave. She batted her eyelids and struck a pose that made her look helpless. "And I need to eat in my condition."

"What condition is that?" Noah said impatiently.

Alice smiled. "Why I'm pregnant, of course."

Maeve wished she'd had sense enough to leave sooner. She could see the battle on Noah's face and she figured his resigned look meant what she thought it did. She was going back to the bedroom until the woman left.

* * *

"Come on in," Noah said. "I'll find you something to eat. You may as well sit down while Jimmy unloads the supplies anyway."

Noah nodded to the boy and Jimmy walked back to the kitchen. He always parked the wagon by the back door so he could unload everything easier.

When he stepped into the kitchen, Noah wondered how he could have missed the smell. Maeve had made bread. The golden loaves sat on the table and he searched a drawer to find a knife to cut into one of them.

"You can sit here," Noah said to the woman who had once been his wife. He used the knife to slice off a thick piece of bread. He knew how much work it was to make bread. And, he had seen that Maeve had made butter, too. He couldn't help but notice that the kitchen was spotless, as well.

He hadn't wanted Maeve to work today, but he liked to see that she had taken charge.

His ex-wife ate the bread quickly and held out her hand for more.

"Why'd you come back really?" Noah asked as he cut another slice of the bread. "If you're carrying the judge's baby, shouldn't you be staying with him?"

"I can't," the woman said, her voice distressed. "I just can't."

For the first time since she'd started talking, Noah believed there was something genuine in her protest.

As he was quiet for a moment, he could hear Jimmy unloading the supplies into the cabinets out in the small room off the kitchen.

"This judge—he doesn't beat you or anything, does he?"

She shook her head. "He's actually rather sweet."

"Good, because I would report him to the sheriff if he was beating you."

She looked surprised. "There was a time when you would have gone in person to persuade him."

Noah shrugged. "I suppose there was."

They were silent for a moment.

"I changed my name to Alice for you," the woman said then. "I know you never liked Allison. You said it was out of place here in the territories. That it belonged in a big city like San Francisco."

"I never meant you should change it. Your name is your name."

Allison nodded. "I'll be a better wife to you this time."

Noah stood up. "I'm sure we'd do lots of things differently, but it's not going to happen—getting back together. You're someone else's wife, bound and legal. I couldn't face God if I took another man's wife from him."

"Oh, you always were too religious for your own good," Allison said impatiently.

"You can wait in here," Noah said as he started

walking toward the door. "I'm going to help Jimmy get our supplies put in place."

With that, he left the house.

In the bedroom, Maeve heard the back door slam and assumed everyone had left again. She needed to keep an eye on the stew and she wanted to make some sugar cookies for the ranch hands to take with them tomorrow if they had to ride out again. She thought she had all the ingredients and the stove needed to be hot for the stew anyway.

Maeve didn't see the woman sitting at the table until she'd taken several steps into the kitchen. She could tell the woman hadn't heard her coming in and Maeve was tempted to leave, but then she saw the way the woman's shoulders were slumped down in despair. Maeve had felt that way not long ago and she couldn't leave someone else as forgotten as she'd felt.

"Can I help you?" Maeve said softly as she walked over and sat down in a chair. "Alice, isn't it?"

"Oh, what difference does my name make?" the woman said as she dabbed at the tears sliding down her face. "I changed it to Alice to please Noah, but he doesn't care. My real name is Allison. I could be named Matilda and he wouldn't care."

It was only because Maeve could feel the woman's distress that she reached over and patted her shoulder. "You must love Noah very much to do something like that."

"Humph," the woman said in disgust. "I wish I did."

"Well, then why did you do it?" Maeve asked in surprise.

"I love my judge," she said. "But I can't live poor. We've always had a servant to help me. My judge doesn't know I can't cook. I can't sew. I can't clean. And I can't bear to tell him. And my baby—what will I do for my baby?"

More tears rolled down Allison's face. "I thought I could come back to Noah. He can always get one of the ranch hands to do the cooking. And no one cares about sewing here. The men all take care of their own buttons. My other husband can find a wife who knows how to do that kind of thing."

Maeve felt a bubble of relief float up inside her. She almost started to laugh.

"You mean this is all about cooking?" Maeve asked, feeling considerably better than she had earlier. "And mending clothes?"

"A man puts a great deal of store on having a meal that's properly prepared. And his shirt in good order."

"I can teach you," Maeve offered. "Cooking is not hard after you've had someone show you the way. And anyone can sew on a button."

"You'd do that for me?" Allison asked as more tears flowed down her cheeks. "After I was so mean to you? I knew you were Noah's new mail-order bride. I just didn't want to admit he was replacing me with a woman he didn't even know." She stopped. "Oh, I didn't mean that the way it sounded. I'm sure he loves you and is looking forward to living his life with you."

Maeve blinked back tears of her own. "He doesn't know if he wants to marry me. My daughter, Violet, and I are just staying until he can figure out what to do."

Allison reached over and put her hand over Maeve's.

"Don't you worry," she said. "I can help you with Noah if you help me learn to cook and sew. Just even a little would make me think I could do it."

"We'll need to ask Noah if you can stay a day or two," Maeve said. "I haven't been upstairs yet, but I'm sure there's a spare bedroom up there."

"Please, just don't tell Noah I'm learning how to cook," Allison asked.

Maeve shrugged. "I won't, unless you say I can."

"Thanks." Allison smiled and stood up. "I'll get Jimmy to bring my bag inside. Noah won't turn me away when I tell him I need to stay for the baby."

Maeve nodded, realizing she couldn't tell Noah about her baby now. He might think she was copying Allison and trying to get the attention from him that the other woman was receiving. But it would be only a couple of days, she thought, as she watched

Allison open the door to where the supplies were being unloaded.

All would work out well, though, Maeve assured herself as she stood. If Allison did know how to convince Noah to marry, it would be the answer to Maeve's problem, too. In the meantime, she would go upstairs to see if she could find sheets for the bed she hoped was there for Allison.

Chapter Seven

That night, Noah was sitting in a chair at the bunkhouse. The windows showed it was dark outside except for the faint light coming from the full moon that was overhead. Most of the ranch hands were there, too, still reminiscing about the supper they'd just had. He wished he'd been able to enjoy it as much as the others. He had been too taken aback by the request he'd gotten from both women to savor his meal. Why had the women asked for Allison to stay two days? He didn't want to appear inhospitable in front of Maeve, but he didn't trust Allison to leave when she was supposed to if he agreed she could stay.

He had nodded his agreement, though, and now wished he hadn't. Christmas was coming and he wanted to spend every minute with Maeve and Violet that he could.

"I haven't had butter like that since my mother

was alive," Bobby said for the fifth time. He was lying on his bunk and staring at the ceiling as though he could see a picture of the meal up there. "And that bread—has anyone ever had bread that good?"

Several of the men said they hadn't. Between all of them, they'd eaten the full ten loaves.

"My mother couldn't cook at all," another ranch hand said. "But she tried. She never made anything like those cookies, though."

Noah was getting restless. "Mothers will do anything for their children."

The ranch hands nodded.

Maybe Maeve had agreed to Allison staying because of the baby, Noah decided. Women were like that. He was glad to find that Maeve was generous, but he didn't think she knew that his decision would only encourage Allison to think he might marry her again. He would never do that no matter how many divorces she received.

"We've got an expectant mother in the house," Noah mentioned then.

He hadn't expected the eruption of cheers.

"So she finally told you, did she?" Dakota asked. "I know it's a secret, but I had to tell the other guys. We're all family anyway."

The older ranch hand was more like a brother than an employee to Noah so he was surprised to learn something new about him. "I never knew you liked Allison so well."

"Allison?" The grin left Dakota's face. "What's she got to do with it?"

"Well, it's her baby," Noah said.

"It can't be," Dakota maintained firmly.

"That's what she says," Noah told him, more than a little curious at the bleak expression on the older man's face. Having everyone's beard shaved off meant Noah was able to tell the emotions of his ranch hands more easily. And they could probably sense more of his feelings, too. This wasn't necessarily good, he told himself.

"Allison always was a liar," Dakota said as he stood up. "I'm going for a walk."

The man put on his hat, took his coat off its peg and left the bunkhouse.

"I hope he's not going over to the house to get another cookie," Bobby said as he sat up on his bed. "They're supposed to be shared. Maeve said."

"I doubt that's what he's doing." Noah stood, too. "But a walk sounds good."

Noah put on his coat and hat and then opened the door. It was cold outside and a gust of wind blew in before he walked through and closed the door behind him. The moon lit the path from the barn to the house, and Noah could see Dakota knocking on the back door of the kitchen. A light shone in the dining area so Noah figured one or both of the women were there, maybe sitting at the table talking.

That's when it hit him. The only thing those two

women had in common was him. They were likely sitting as Allison went over a list of his faults. Surely, it couldn't take two full days to go through his many failings, but he suspected that was the reason Allison wanted to stay. She was going to warn Maeve off.

Even though, as he reminded himself, he was the one who wanted to give Maeve time to decide if she wanted to stay with him, he still didn't feel as if someone else should be speaking against him.

When he followed the path past the windows of the house, he looked over and saw that he'd been right. The frost stopped him from seeing things clearly, but he could make out Maeve and Allison sitting at the table, a lantern in the middle. They were holding sewing needles. Maeve had a pile of socks in front of her and Allison had an old shirt he kept in the downstairs closet and a pile of buttons.

He'd never thought to see Allison mending one of his cast-off shirts.

When he took a step forward, he saw that neither woman was paying attention to her needle. They were both looking up at Dakota.

Noah decided he better get inside. He didn't bother with knocking since, as he reminded himself, it was his house.

Noah took his boots off in the entry to spare the clean floors.

He walked quietly in his socks, but when he got near the table, he saw that Allison was the only one there. She was bent over that shirt of his and appeared to be intent on pulling the threaded needle through a stitch of some kind.

"Where's Maeve?" he demanded as he stood behind her.

"Ooooh!" she screeched a little as she let the shirt drop to the table and put a hand up to her chest before turning around to face him. "You scared me."

"I'm sorry, but Maeve was just here," he continued. "I want to know where she is, that's all."

Allison cocked her head and looked at him for a minute before starting to smile.

"You like her," she said then with what appeared to be satisfaction in her voice.

Noah didn't answer. He was never surprised any longer when Allison pretended to have feelings she didn't have. "I just want to talk to her for a minute."

At that moment, he heard a door open in the hallway to his left and turned. Maeve was coming out of the parlor and Dakota was following right behind her.

"He wants to talk to you," Allison said to Maeve with the smile still on her face. "So if you will excuse me, I think I'll go up to bed."

With that, Allison stood up, stuck her needle in the old shirt and folded it up.

Noah noticed then that there were a dozen buttons sewn onto that shirt. He'd worn the shirt one year for branding and there were already several burned holes in the cloth. It was puzzling, but he was too intent on talking to Maeve to worry about an old shirt.

Dakota lingered a little longer than Allison, but he finally gave Noah an abrupt nod and started walking to the door. When he stood in the doorway, he turned.

"Remember the reverend," he warned.

He closed the door behind him before Noah could respond.

By that time, Maeve had sat back down at the table and taken up her needle again.

"I don't recognize those socks," Noah said as he sat down. He figured he should talk with her for a while before he demanded to know what Allison had told her about him. He was growing more curious though. There were white socks, brown ones and a couple of green ones.

"They belonged to my husband," Maeve said as she picked up a white sock.

"And you're mending them?"

She shook her head. "I'm making a sock doll for Violet for Christmas. At least, I hope it's done by then."

She held up the stocking. "They all have holes in them, though. I didn't realize how bad my husband's socks were until he died. I'm going to cut out the best parts of each one and sew them together. That's what's going to take so long."

"You're welcome to use some of my socks," Noah offered.

"I couldn't," Maeve said as she shook her head.

They were both silent for a moment.

"I'm sure Violet will appreciate her doll," Noah finally said.

Maeve set down the sock she was working on.

"I hope she does," she said and then smiled at him. "You know how children are. She'll appreciate the sentiment of the doll when she's older, but right now she has her heart set on something fancier."

"Ah," Noah said sympathetically.

He didn't bother to admit that he had no idea what children were like. But he did remember the conversation Maeve and her daughter had had in front of the mercantile. He'd originally thought it was the teapot that interested them, but it was the doll.

"I hope it's not too much for you to have Allison here," Noah said. "I know you're probably feeling like you have to help her because of the baby, but you don't need to."

"I'm not worried about her baby," Maeve said.

Noah nodded. "I just want you to be happy. There's not much time until Christmas and I'm sure you want to do some things for Violet."

"She doesn't expect much," Maeve said softly. "But she has wanted to have a decorated tree. I don't see any pine trees around here, though."

"I know where there's a scrub tree in a ravine

near here that would look like a pine if I trimmed it a little," Noah said. "I could ride out and get it, if you want. I'm planning to ride into Miles City tomorrow, but I could get the tree on the next day."

"The twenty-third?"

Noah nodded. "Unless you need it sooner."

"That would be a fine day to have the tree," Maeve said, looking pleased.

"We never did decorate a tree," Noah said. "So we don't have any decorations. I could buy some in Miles City if you want, though."

"Oh, no," Maeve said. "We can make our own. String some popcorn. Make some cutout cookies to hang. If we have some white paper, we can cut out some shapes of angels to hang. Even pieces of red ribbon will do."

"I have paper in my office upstairs. You're welcome to take what you need."

Maeve was silent for a moment, worrying her lips.

"Do you think the ranch hands would want to help with the decorating?" she asked. "That would make it seem more like a party for Violet."

Noah grinned. "I can't think of anything they would like better unless it would be for you to do the inviting so they know they are truly welcome."

He could not remember one time when Allison had invited his men into their home for anything like a party. They were never the kind of society folks that she wanted to entertain.

"Maybe we should have an early dinner on the twenty-fourth instead of the twenty-third," Maeve said. "Then we can decorate the tree and eat cookies. That will give me a couple of days to get everything else ready."

"I don't want you to go to too much trouble now," Noah cautioned her as he stood to leave. "And, I want you to know that if you have any questions about me, you can ask me."

Maeve nodded, but he didn't think she understood.

Still, as he stood there in the lantern light and looked over at Maeve as she sat there with her copper hair tamed into waves around her face and her eyes looking at him kindly, he wanted her to do more than just think well of him.

He stepped closer and put his hand on her shoulder.

"I didn't thank you enough for dinner," he said.

"It was my pleasure," she whispered as she looked up at him, her face shining with joy at his compliment.

"You're a genuinely good woman," he said then as he bent down and kissed her forehead. "I want you to know I—ah—think highly of you."

Noah realized he should have thought about what to say before he stepped into the kitchen. He had never been good with talking about his emotions, though.

Just then a thin cry came from the bedroom. "Mommy."

"I have to go," Maeve said as she stood up.

"I know."

Noah watched her hurry out of the room. Then he turned to leave. For the first time he could remember, he was looking forward to Christmas.

The next morning, Maeve was standing at the cookstove before Dakota came into the kitchen. She had pancake batter stirred and bacon sizzling on the stove. The rest of the eggs in the basin were sitting nearby, ready to be cracked.

"You don't really mean the ranch hands can't have any more eggs, do you?" she asked the older man as she spooned pancake batter onto a flat skillet. "Because, if you did, I'm only going to fry one a piece."

He shook his head. "No, I was just trying to make a point to Noah."

"I figured as much," she said, reaching for the platter she was going to keep the pancakes on while she waited for all the ranch hands to get to the table.

"That man has a hard head," Dakota added.

Maeve smiled. She liked hearing the affection in the men's voices when they talked about Noah. "I noticed as much."

"He's a good man," the ranch hand continued and then stopped in thought for a minute. "He just—Well, he worries about disappointing people. Like when he was married to Allison. He was bringing cattle onto this land, but he wasn't making much money. Any fool could see he was going to come out all right, but Allison didn't have time to wait."

"She didn't love him enough," Maeve said as she flipped the pancakes and took the bacon out of the skillets.

Dakota grunted. "That's the truth."

"I think he might like me, but I don't know," Maeve said, turning her face toward the stove so she didn't have to see the expression on the older man's face.

"I'd say he does," Dakota said thoughtfully. "It would help if Allison wasn't here, though."

"If he wants to be with her, I'd rather know it," Maeve said as she started cracking eggs. "She's a beautiful woman."

"I don't think that's it," Dakota said as he absentmindedly stepped closer to her and helped crack the eggs. "Allison just reminds him of his failures. Makes him reluctant to try again."

They were busy cracking the eggs and putting them in one of the skillets to fry so they didn't talk for a few minutes.

"I haven't told him about the baby yet," Maeve finally confessed when all the food was cooking. "And he's going to Miles City today so he'll be gone. In fact, I think he already left. I heard a horse walk past the window earlier."

"His room is empty at the bunkhouse," Dakota said, agreeing. "Leaving as early as he did, though, he'll be home for supper."

"I hope so," Maeve said. "I plan to make an announcement—"

Dakota looked up.

"Not about the baby," she assured him. "I want to invite all of the ranch hands for a Christmas Eve party to decorate the tree."

"We're going to have a tree?" Dakota asked, his eyes wide with wonder.

Maeve nodded her head. "With popcorn strings and gingerbread men. Red ribbon and pinecones, if we can find any. I'll start making the cookies tomorrow."

"Well, I'll be..." Dakota's voice trailed off. "We're going to have a regular Christmas."

Maeve nodded. "But don't tell anyone until supper."

Breakfast was subdued, the men all eating solemnly like they couldn't quite get used to everything. The pancakes were golden, the bacon crisp and brown, and the eggs were cooked to perfection.

The ranch hands left with a thankful chorus, leaving Maeve and Allison at the table.

"You haven't told me what Noah wanted last night," Allison said as she pushed her chair closer to Maeve.

"Not much," Maeve said and then hesitated. "I think he might like me, but I'm not sure."

Allison leaned back and examined Maeve critically.

"Maybe it's the servant's uniform," she said. "You need to make a man sit up and take notice. They like their women to dress pretty."

"But I don't have anything else, except my church dress and that's gray."

"I can help you with that," Allison said as she smiled. "I can spare one of my dresses for you to wear to the Christmas Eve party."

"I'm taller than you," Maeve reminded the woman.

"We can make some adjustments," Allison said.

Maeve wasn't sure what the other woman had in mind, but she was willing to find out. After all, the two of them had an agreement. Maeve was teaching her how to be a useful wife with all the cooking and sewing lessons. Allison was in charge of getting Noah's attention.

Chapter Eight

It took two days for Maeve and Allison to get everything ready for the party on Christmas Eve, but the time was finally almost there. The two of them were sitting at the table, each with a cup of hot tea in front of them. Breakfast had been over for hours and they had been making the final arrangements for the party since them.

Maeve couldn't have done everything alone and she was grateful for Allison's help.

Violet had been skipping around the house all that time, too, playing with her pillow doll and the sprig of mistletoe from the train. She'd gone to the parlor to tell her doll about the "misty toe," as she called it.

"She's got quite an imagination," Allison said.

Maeve nodded.

"Did you ever finish the sock doll?" the other woman asked.

Maeve shook her head. "For some reason, watching the needle go back and forth makes me queasy. But I have two nice handkerchiefs I plan to give Violet. She'll like those."

Yesterday, Maeve had told Allison that she was pregnant, too. She'd had no choice when she couldn't prepare breakfast for the men. The other woman, under Maeve's direction, had taken over more of the cooking since then and was feeling justifiably proud.

"I'm glad I've been spared that," Allison said with a shudder. "Morning sickness."

"I didn't have it the first couple of months, either," Maeve said. "So take advantage of the fact that you don't have it yet and travel back to Denver to be with your husband while you can."

"Not until I find a way to go back gracefully," Allison said. "If I start back by apologizing I'll be doing it for the rest of my life."

"Better to lose your pride than your husband," Maeve advised.

Allison grinned, but she didn't say anything.

Just then Violet ran into the kitchen.

"Someone's coming," she announced. "With a wagon and a big horse."

Maeve asked Allison if she could answer the front door, and the other woman took pity on her. Violet followed down the hallway, and Maeve was left alone in the kitchen. She looked around her in satisfaction. Everything was ready for the party.

The tree was in the root cellar with its trunk in a bucket of rocks and water. Noah was going to bring it in soon. More than a hundred gingerbread cookies were lying on the table with pieces of red yarn tied through them so they could be hung on the branches. The golden corn kernels were ready for popping and Allison had threaded two dozen needles so everyone could start making a garland when the kernels were puffed white.

Maeve had never had a large party like this, and it had cheered everyone in the house up more than she had expected. There was only an hour until the ranch hands would be coming over. Dakota had already told her that they'd been heating hot water for days, between the baths and the shirts that needed to be washed. Of course, they had all shaved, too.

She had peeled potatoes earlier and they had a hearty potato soup simmering. Maeve had made sourdough bread for supper after they finished with the tree. They'd decorate the house some, too, and then Maeve was serving a peach cobbler with coffee and tea.

The big Christmas meal, ham and some dried apple pies, would be at noon tomorrow.

Noah was giving the ranch hands most of today and tomorrow off. Just the animal chores would be done—feeding the cattle, milking the cows and gathering the eggs.

Maeve had heard whispers that some of the men

liked to sing and had been practicing Christmas songs for the past few days. They had hesitated to offer to entertain everyone when they knew Allison was still going to be there, but Maeve convinced them that the other woman would enjoy their efforts, too.

The men had started coming by the kitchen periodically during the day, each one with a compliment about Noah. She didn't tell them, but their effort touched her deeply. She wished she had listened to what other people said when she'd gotten married the first time. Noah himself had also been by, helping her tie yarn bows on the gingerbread men and reaching up to the high shelves to find the dried apples.

Just then, Maeve heard footsteps coming down the hall and she told herself she needed to stop letting her mind wander.

Allison was the first one back into the kitchen, obviously flustered with her cheeks pink and her eyes sparkling. A distinguished gentleman with a mustache and a cane followed her.

"This is my husband," she said breathlessly. "He came all this way to get me."

The man nodded his head toward Maeve. "May I thank you for taking care of my wife until I could get here. I did not know she was with child until your husband sent me a telegram."

"Noah?" Maeve said and then squeaked in alarm.

"Oh, he's not my husband. It's just that this is his house."

The man smiled and bowed slightly. "Allison tells me your name is Maeve Flanagan. I'm Judge Brandon Scott—soon to be reinstated, I hope. I'm pleased to meet you."

Maeve had never met a judge of any kind before so she gave a slight curtsy.

She had no sooner finished than the back door opened and Noah came inside.

"You made it," he said as he walked forward and held out his hand to the judge. "And in good time, too."

"I'm in your debt," the man said. "I did not know where to look until I got your telegram."

Noah inclined his head. "I was glad to do it."

Maeve was relieved the preparations were almost ready for tonight. She knew from looking at her that Allison would want to spend the rest of the day with her husband.

"You're staying for the party, aren't you?" Maeve asked the judge.

"In this kind of weather, you won't be able travel until morning anyway," Noah added. "And we have plenty of room."

"Please, Brandie," Allison added.

The judge looked pleased and nodded. "Very well."

Then he looked down at his wife with an expression of such adoration on his face that Maeve felt a stab of jealousy go right through to her heart.

Noah reached over and took her hand. Together they walked down the hall to the parlor, leaving the other couple standing there.

Violet was in the room, sitting on the floor playing with her pillow doll, but she stood up when Noah and Maeve entered.

"Could you go in the bedroom and give your doll a nap?" Maeve asked her daughter. Maybe now was the time to have a conversation with Noah.

Violet wasn't looking at Noah as if she was afraid of him, but she was not rushing toward him, either. She nodded her head at her mother and carried the doll out of the parlor.

"I'm sorry," Maeve began and then faltered. Noah must have realized she had something serious to say since his face was solemn.

"What do you have to be sorry about?" Noah asked softly.

"Looking at Allison and her husband makes me realize I want that, too," Maeve said. That wasn't what she thought she was going to say, but the words seemed to come forth on their own.

"You want to be loved," Noah said, his voice neither rising nor falling. It was completely flat.

"I know that's not what you advertised for," Maeve continued. The words were not going the way she had planned, but her heart wouldn't let her change course.

"I thought I was past wanting someone to love me and not just take care of me. But you were right. It's not enough for a lifetime."

Noah studied her for a minute. "I thought you were going to finally tell me that you're pregnant."

"You know?"

Noah nodded. "I finally figured it out."

"And that's another reason," Maeve said, blinking back tears. "You only have room for one child."

"I said I was an only child, not that I wouldn't accept a baby also."

Maeve nodded. "I'm going to ask Allison and the judge if Violet and I can go back to Denver with them. There will be lots of jobs for a widow woman in a big city like that."

With that, she turned and walked out of the room.

Noah stood there, stunned. None of this was supposed to happen. He'd thought she would stay.

And then, as clear as if she was in the room with him, he remembered Mrs. Barker telling him with some urgency in her voice that he needed to share his feelings if he was going to keep his marriage to Allison.

He hadn't been willing then. But now—he ran out of the parlor and down the hall.

There was no one in the kitchen or the dining room. Allison and her husband must have gone upstairs. That left only his bedroom. He raced back down the hall and knocked on the door. He figured the reverend would have to forgive him because Noah knew this was not acceptable.

But Maeve, bless her heart, answered his knock.

She'd been crying; her cheeks were pink and wet. Her glorious hair was swirling about her.

"What do you want?" she said, her voice thick and unhappy.

"You," he said. "I want you."

She just looked at him.

Then she looked behind her at Violet and gestured for him to step out into the hall. She shut the door and followed him.

He knelt at her feet.

"I want to tell you everything about me," he said as he looked up. "How abandoned I felt when my parents died. How alone I was in the care of my aunts. How I resented God and didn't think I could ever love anyone again. How I made a mockery of my marriage to Allison. How my wife left me because I couldn't seem to care enough. And how much I've come to love you."

He stopped for breath.

He didn't know what he would say next to convince Maeve to stay. And then he saw her bend down slowly until she was on her knees, too.

"I want to tell you," she began. "How my husband destroyed my faith in love. How he betrayed me with other women. How he made me ashamed to go to church. How I blamed him and blamed him and never once asked myself if I could have stopped him. If I could have prayed for him more. Loved him more. I ran away from the scandal and was still hiding. And, to make it worse, I was so angry at God that I told myself He was angry with me. And then I want to say how much I love you, too."

She stopped talking then, and Noah did what was natural. He leaned across to her and rested his forehead against hers.

"We have a lot of talking to do," he said softly. "A lifetime of talking."

He could see the smile start to curve her lips. That's when he kissed her.

He was starting to kiss her for a second time when he heard the outside door to the kitchen open.

"The men are coming for supper," Maeve whispered.

"They've missed meals before," Noah said. He didn't want to move from where they were.

"But it's the party, too," Maeve reminded him.

They rose up together and held hands as they walked down the hall. It was only when they got to the kitchen that Maeve remembered her daughter.

"Violet," she gasped as she turned. "I'll be right back."

Noah let her go and turned to greet the ranch hands.

They were all standing there, beaming at him.

"You were mighty cozy there," Dakota said.

Noah grinned. "I'm not going to wait any longer. I'm going to marry her if she'll have me."

"You mean you haven't asked her yet?" Dakota demanded.

Noah laughed out right. "I guess I have. With the ad and all. But I want to do it proper and from the heart."

The party started right then, Noah thought, even though Maeve and Allison insisted they weren't dressed yet so he kept an eye on Violet and started the ranch hands on the popcorn strings. A couple of the men were humming Christmas carols until everyone joined in.

Maeve and Allison came down the hall at the same time.

Half of the men whistled, but Noah didn't have the breath for it. He thought his heart had stopped. Maeve was wearing a green silk dress, with tucks pulling the waist in and a scooped neckline that made her neck look elegant. Allison was wearing a red dress, and together they looked like Christmas.

"You're beautiful," he said as he walked close enough to Maeve to capture her hand again.

He was staring at her, he knew, but he couldn't seem to stop. And then Violet was standing next to him and saying something about being lifted up. He looked down. There was no fear on her face as she asked to be taken up. He bent down and did so.

She no sooner had she gotten up in his arms than she started to giggle and lift one arm high in an attempt to get something over his head.

"Misty toe," Violet said in triumph. "You can't kiss without some misty toe."

Noah decided the girl had the right idea. He leaned forward and kissed Maeve until she was breathless.

"Will you marry me?" he asked while her eyes were still soft and unfocused.

She smiled. "Yes."

A cheer erupted from the ranch hands, and there was much slapping of one another on the back. In fact, the party was in such high spirits that Noah decided it was time for Violet to receive her Christmas present.

"I think we have another guest for the party," he said to Violet, who was still in his arms talking about her "misty toe."

He had put her present on the top shelf of the entry into the kitchen, and he carried her out there now, with Maeve following.

Violet went silent when she looked at the doll on the shelf.

"For me?" she finally asked.

"All for you," Noah assured her.

"You didn't need to," Maeve said beside him.

"But I wanted to," Noah told her.

Even though Violet was too busy to raise up her

mistletoe, Noah figured it was a good time for a kiss and leaned over to Maeve.

"I'm glad you finally stopped kissing me on the cheek," Maeve said after she got her breath back.

"Me, too," Noah said. "Me, too."

Epilogue

Near the Dry Creek in Montana Territory
July 1887

The hot heat of summer made Maeve fan herself with a piece of paper. It was a Sunday afternoon and grasshoppers were jumping around. The ranch hands had loaded the benches and chairs from the bunkhouse into a wagon and driven them over to the banks of the Dry Creek so everyone would have a place to sit for the baptism. Maeve was grateful for that as she sat on one of them with her baby son, Charles, on her lap. The church was having a baptism in the creek and, while Charles was too young for that, she and Noah wanted to dedicate him to the Lord this Sunday.

She glanced next to her where her friend Mercy and her husband, Cole Matheson, were sitting. Maeve had asked them to be godparents to Charles, and they had taken the train back here from Angel Falls to do so. She and Mercy wrote to each other almost weekly and had become solid friends.

Noah was sitting next to Maeve in a new suit, and he couldn't be prouder of Charles.

"Good lungs," he'd said when the baby was born. "He'll make a good rancher."

Mercy leaned over and whispered, "You should have told me you were pregnant on the train." She'd made the same statement several times before. "I can't imagine how alone and afraid you felt."

"It all worked out," Maeve said as she reached over and squeezed her friend's hand.

Mercy, too, had found love in her mail-order match. And she was now pregnant and waiting for another child.

"I wish I could go back and thank that conductor," Mercy said.

With that thought, they both looked over to the grassy area to their left. Violet had found a sprig of some kind of wild grass that she was calling her "misty toe." She was chasing Mercy's son, George, around in circles trying to get him to kiss her.

"She's five now you know," Maeve said to Mercy. "So she's a little faster."

"George can still outrun her for quite a few years

more years," Mercy said with a grin. "Maybe then kissing won't seem so bad."

That was all the conversation they had before Reverend Olson came forward with those who wanted to be baptized in the creek.

Bobby was the first one in line and Noah smiled over at Maeve. She hadn't realized that the boy had been with Noah's crew since he was fourteen. He was eighteen now. Noah had encouraged him all those years to read his Bible and go to church. He had recently turned to God completely.

Finally, it was time for them to go forward with Charles.

Noah carried the baby down to where Reverend Olson stood by the creek. Maeve was by his side and even Violet was there, looking a little rumpled from her chase.

The Mathesons followed behind them.

"We are here to dedicate this precious boy," the Reverend Olson said as he began. "Jesus asked the little children to come to him and this boy is doing that."

After the reverend was finished, Noah carried the baby back to their chairs.

The dedication was the last one and people started bringing out their food for the picnic they were all having.

Maeve noticed that Violet was staying with the adults.

"What's wrong?" she asked her daughter. "Don't you want to play anymore?"

"George won't let me catch him," she said as she folded her arms in a temper.

"Well, sometimes you have to wait for the good kisses," Maeve said as she bent down and gave her daughter a big one on her cheek.

Noah chuckled beside her and when Maeve straightened up, he leaned over and kissed her cheek, too.

"Sometimes you don't have to wait as long as you think, either," Noah said.

* * * * *

Dear Reader,

Welcome back to the third holiday mail-order bride book by Jillian Hart and myself.

As many of you know, I love Christmas stories so I am pleased to be able to offer you another story for this year. *Mistletoe Kiss in Dry Creek* is the story of a recent widow, Maeve Flanagan, who believes God has abandoned her and left her with no choice but to go West to marry a stranger.

I always try to include some mention of loneliness or distance from God in my holiday books because, each year, some of you send me letters that tell me you have felt that way at Christmas and a book of mine has encouraged you.

This year, I hope you enjoy Maeve's story as she goes to meet the man who placed an ad for a wife even though all he wants is one who can cook for his ranch hands. Fortunately, her young daughter, Violet, is determined her mother will have a Christmas kiss under the mistletoe with him.

Thank you for reading my *Mistletoe Kiss in Dry Creek.*

I wish you an especially meaningful Christmas this year. May you find time to gather with other Christians to sing carols and remember the Holy Birth.

Janet Tronstad

Questions for Discussion

1. In the beginning of the novella, Maeve is convinced God has abandoned her. Have you ever felt that so much was wrong with your life that God had turned His face from you? If you could have talked to Maeve then, what would you have told her? Does God allow difficult things to happen to His children?

2. Noah, on the other hand, seems to be frozen in his feelings. He had hard times, too, but he chose to just work as much as he could, hoping the feelings would go away. What would have been a better way for him to cope with the hard times in his life?

3. The railroad conductor gives both Maeve and her friend Mercy sprigs of mistletoe in hopes they will have Christmas kisses from their new husbands. He may have sensed their unease and given them these sprigs for encouragement. When was the last time you gave something to a friend as a means to encourage them?

4. Violet had a traumatic experience and was scared of bearded men. The ranch hands all

had beards. How did they solve this problem? Have you ever made a sacrifice to make some-one else feel better?

COMING NEXT MONTH FROM

Love Inspired® Historical

Available January 7, 2014

CLAIMING THE COWBOY'S HEART

Cowboys of Eden Valley

Linda Ford

Jayne Gardiner is determined never to be a damsel in distress again. But when her shooting lesson goes awry, she must nurse an injured cowboy back on his feet. Will he walk away with her heart?

LONE WOLF'S LADY

Judy Duarte

Outspoken suffragist Katie O'Malley and guarded bounty hunter Tom McCain couldn't be more different. With a child's life in danger these opposites must find a way to work together—or risk losing each other forever!

THE WYOMING HEIR

Naomi Rawlings

Rancher Luke Hayes wants nothing to do with his estranged grandfather's inheritance—or the floundering local girl's school in need of a donation. But will beautiful Elizabeth Wells teach him the importance of family—and love?

JOURNEY OF HOPE

Debbie Kaufman

Even the perils of the Liberian jungle won't discourage missionary Anna Baldwin from fulfilling her calling. It isn't until Stewart Hastings arrives that she realizes the greater danger may be falling for the wounded veteran.

LOOK FOR THESE AND OTHER LOVE INSPIRED BOOKS WHEREVER BOOKS ARE SOLD, INCLUDING MOST BOOKSTORES, SUPERMARKETS, DISCOUNT STORES AND DRUGSTORES.

LIHCNM1213